Marshals of the Unseen

ISBN-9798689609478

Table of Contents

Chapter I

The train pulled into the station breathing smoke and fire like a dragon of black iron, the furnace within it devouring coal with a relentless and mechanical hunger.

Sheriff Annabel stood alone at the small station, her bootheels firmly planted on the uneven old planks of the platform with an unlit cigarette clamped between her lips. A faded and worn stalker hat shielded her face from the morning sun, and a heavy woolen poncho kept the morning chill off of her arms and chest. The train was early, as it always was. Drivers who had to take the old iron serpent to Ganndo Valley were rarely able to grasp how short the trip actually was. There were no other stops after passing the mountain ridge to the east, and the land leading to the valley was even and fair. This stop was the last on the route, the tracks came to a dead end at the valley. The other fork in the line back at Mantis City led farther out west into rougher country that brought promises of wealth and gold with it. Once news spread that the old silver mine near Ganndo Valley was empty and dry, folks ceased caring about expanding the rail for a time. Only recently had the rail companies begun working on expanding the railroad lines to the sleeping frontier town, which was being done with little more motivation than casual testament to "manifest destiny." Beyond this place was a wild, empty expanse of unsettled frontier that was just beginning to be explored.

Brakes squealed as the engine car slowed to a stop, and the train's whistle blew twice, loudly echoing over the valley. Heavy metal wheels ground down to a halt upon the tracks until the great machine came to rest beside the station.

After a time, a few of the townsfolk who had deliveries to collect from the locomotive would be getting ready to make the long ride from town to the station, pulling carts and wagons with them to return with their supplies. Annabel was here to collect something of a different sort, and she was not happy about it.

Leaning out of the engine window, the driver tipped his blue hat to the sheriff. As he waved, she could see the brass buttons of his coat twinkling in the sun. Annabel struck a match with a fingernail and lit her cigarette.

"Good morning to you sir," he said, his nose red and his cheeks painted with coal. Annabel lifted her head to greet him, and the man choked for a moment trying to correct himself.

"Oh! Pardon me, ma'am. Good morning to you."

"You've said that already," Annabel said, taking no offense at the conductor's mistake, "Good morning to you as well."

The conductor pulled at a lever and opened the creaking iron door before stepping down from the high car. He brushed his hands off on his overalls and wiped his forehead with a poppy red handkerchief.

"When the marshal said he'd be meeting with the town Sheriff, I just sort of assumed it would be, you know. A, er, a gentleman."

Annabel shook her head, marveling at the man's continued efforts to make a bigger fool of himself. Strangers often did upon learning the sheriff in these parts was a woman. She dropped the butt of her cigarette and ground the smoldering thing into the boards of the platform with her heel. Bunting flapped in the gentle breeze that hung from the station's overhang.

"He planning on coming out anytime soon?"

"Truthfully, ma'am, I think he's asleep."

The sheriff scowled in an ugly way. Typical. She had experience working with outside law before from bigger cities in the east. Men with clean and soft hands who didn't know anything about trail craft, who couldn't name more than a handful of the people that lived and died in the territories they policed. As law, they were too separate from the communities they were sworn to protect in Annabel's opinion.

Annabel checked her watch. Nearly half past six. She snapped her watch shut so abruptly that it made the conductor jump.

"What's your name, partner?" she asked the man.

"Daniels. George Daniels, ma'am."

"Mr. Daniels, I don't plan on spending the next hour standing on this platform waiting for the marshal, and I'm not about to waste time with him while a girl has gone missing," she said impatiently. "The first few days are important with things like this. When you see the marshal, you point him in the direction of town. With any luck he'll get lost or give up."

As Annabel walked away from the platform to saddle up, she found her left hand had made its way into her pocket. Tense fingers were wrapping tightly around the letter from the marshal's office, notarized by one Nathaniel Barret. News of a local tragedy in Ganndo Valley had reached their offices, and the crime bore a similarity to others the marshal's office was investigating. As such, they were sending an officer to assist local law enforcement, meaning Annabel, in apprehending the party responsible for the abduction of a young girl. She walked the short distance to where her horse was tethered and saddled up briskly, pulling at the reins to lead the animal back to town.

It was enough to make Annabel spit, which she did after reading the letter the first time after Lewis Tucker dropped it off at her office. The letter was so *government* it was almost hateful. It was an impersonal, heartless thing that was clinical in its composition. It didn't even mention the girl's name. She was just another number to them, and Annabel could only imagine their actual motives for sending her help she hadn't asked for. She was sure that they were tracking down some criminal or another who abducted women that had a sizeable bounty on his head, and thought he'd retreated to the valley. Government funded bounty hunters. Men who gave little thought to things like community. It made the sheriff's stomach turn with anger.

Without waiting another minute, she spurred her horse forwards and rode off back to the valley.

Twice, while she rode the open plains under cloud-spotted blue skies, Annabel considered turning around. Once, almost immediately after she left the station behind, and the second time about an hour later when she thought about how unneighborly it had been to speak to the train conductor like she did.

In both instances her own stubborn streak kept her riding straight on through to the valley. If this outsider really wanted to help her find Rosanna, then it wouldn't matter if he had an escort from the station or not.

She rode into town under the large timber frame that read in painted black letters *Ganndo Valley*. Her horse trotted past quiet buildings and down the dirt roads, kicking up dust as it cantered towards the stables. Around her the townsfolk smiled and waved, even Old Bill, dressed in his old army jacket and half asleep on his rocker gave her a nod. As she closed in on the stable, she started noticing strange reactions from the people around her and turned in the saddle to see what the fuss was about.

Riding into town on a horse-shaped shadow, was a stranger.

At first the sheriff was somewhat startled by the sight. To have arrived this soon after herself meant the man had to have ridden fairly close on the trail, yet she neither heard nor saw any sight of him on her ride. As she looked at the man in the saddle, she felt a distinct feeling of what she could only call *otherness* from him. He and his horse were oddities that almost directly conflicted with one another.

The animal itself was perhaps the most beautiful horse Annabel had ever seen, with a shimmering coat of obsidian that glimmered in the morning sun. Before Annabel could get a better look at the horse, she thought it prudent to take a measure of the man atop the strange and elegant creature.

His suit was an unremarkable three-piece of plain grey cotton over a white shirt and a black looping tie that looked almost comically generic, but immaculately styled. He wore plain black leather boots that had been shined vigorously before his ride, which now already wore a thin layer of dust over them. His gun belt was a similar black leather with a brass buckle, which had gleaming new cartridges looped into it. The plain unadorned holster at his hip held a revolver with a mesquite handle, which had been coated with a smooth resin finish. His face was tanned, which surprised the sheriff. Both his hair and mustache were boot polish black, and his eyes were very dark, almost looking black themselves in the morning sun. He smiled widely at the people as he rode by, greeting them like a politician. He looked almost like a traveling salesman, superficial and personable, ready to tell folks all about the newest cure-all for warts or an elixir for balding men to grow their hair back. Everything about him appeared to be nothing more than a calculated and dishonest veneer.

Already Annabel didn't like him.

She visibly recoiled when she saw Mrs. Mattingly fan herself while the marshal spoke to her from horseback, talking as much with the movements of his hands as with his voice. She laughed and tittered like a schoolchild at almost every word he said before, to Annabel's horror, pointing at the sheriff.

The marshal nodded and winked, by gumption the man actually *winked* at Mrs. Mattingly, before riding in Annabel's direction.

Annabel waited in the saddle until the man had ridden up to her, and as he got about a yard away, she was hit with the scent of an overpowering amount of generic cologne. She nearly gagged.

"I'm not seeing a badge," he said with a pearly smile as he raised an eyebrow, "But if that fair woman yonder is telling the truth of it, you must be Sheriff Annabel Hawke. It's a pleasure to make your acquaintance."

The sheriff felt something mean and snide working its way from her head to her lips but decided not to waste her time insulting the man. Instead she took a short breath and forced an absolutely unconvincing smile of her own.

"If we're presuming before saying hello, then you must be the marshal," she said, unable to stop herself from speaking with a drop of venom, "You have me at a disadvantage with your name, though."

The stranger laughed and nodded his head bashfully, while working a hand through his raven hair.

"I suppose that's true. I apologize for being so blunt. Truthfully, I meant no offense by it. It's just a rare treat for me to see places like this still thriving. Most frontier towns are messes of debauchery and violence. You have a beautiful town here, miss. Train station is a little far away from things, but all in all, it's quaint. Not having a rail running alongside town gives it a certain rural charm that has long left where I come from."

"I'd prefer if you call me Annabel or Sheriff," she chided him, "What do I call you?" she asked, more forward this time about asking for his name since he practically swatted the question aside the first time she asked it.

"Marshal will do," he said absentmindedly, "Say, am I to understand you have a saloon in town by the name of *The Rye in the Sky*? And at said saloon, they distill their own whiskey?"

Annabel wasn't able to stop herself this time, and openly frowned at the man. She couldn't tell if he was being rude on purpose or that he was simply a peculiar sort of man, but she racked his focus back to her by raising her voice ever so slightly.

"Marshal, your office didn't send you cross country on a train to visit our saloon. I was under the impression you were sent to help me with tracking down a missing girl."

"That's absolutely correct," he said, with a sincerity that Annabel believed might actually be genuine before becoming very businesslike in his manner, "She's been missing for three days now, after taking into account the time that's passed since we heard about it from a coal trader, and the time it's taken me to reach your delightful little oasis. Her disappearance is not the first time a person has gone missing from the valley, is that right?"

Annabel nodded.

"Usually it's newcomers who are gamblers or drifters. Sometimes younger folk get an itch in their boots and want to head east," she said, "They want to see cities or the ocean or just set out to make their own way. But this is different. I *know* her, Marshal. Rosanna isn't the kind of girl to leave without saying goodbye."

"Goodbyes can be difficult," the marshal said, leading his horse towards the stable. Annabel followed.

"She would have told someone."

"These other people who have left, do they always tell someone?" he asked with an uncomfortable accusatory tone. Annabel glared at the man like a viper.

"No. What's your point?" she asked him sharply.

"My point, dear Sheriff Annabel, is that in this case we have to start somewhere. The young girl has no family, correct?"

"She does. Her folks moved out to Rue Gri a few years ago. I haven't been able to reach them by mail or wire," Annabel pulled her horse to block the marshal before he rode into the stable. His own horse glared at Annabel hatefully, which startled the sheriff. Up close it was still beautiful, but there was something cruel and sinister about the animal that made the sheriff's hackles itch.

"I am aware of that," the marshal said gently in an inappropriate and almost somber tone, "In my line of work, I have to go from place-to-place to conduct my investigations. Regrettably, I don't have the luxury of serving a stable community of friends and neighbors. I have to rely on the help and kindness of strangers, while *being* a stranger myself, which isn't always welcome in personal matters like this one."

Annabel looked at the horn of her saddle, reluctantly understanding what the man said.

"Where does the *Rye* come into it?"

"What place in any town sees the most traffic?" he asked with a grin, "Which place in *any* town knows where the hotel beds are the softest, or where the prices for a meal are fair?"

"The saloon," Annabel admitted, following the man's logic eventually. He spoke so oddly. If he had started by mentioning his reasons for wanting to visit the saloon, it would have made more sense and the two of them could have skipped their inane dialog. The man clearly thought himself to be either very clever or very interesting, and Annabel found both him and his manner of speaking to be neither of those things.

"The *best* saloon in a town is the place for such matters," the marshal said with a knowing grin, "And since the valley, as you call it, only has the one saloon, that is our best bet to talk to folks who may have heard or seen something. And I confess, I am powerfully thirsty after such a long ride."

"Marshal it's not yet ten in the morning."

"I suppose," the strange lawman sighed with disappointment, "I'll of course have to arrange lodging for myself, and have to speak to your stablemaster for boarding my mount while I'm here. I don't suppose you have any recommendations where a man could get a decent plate of pancakes or johnnycakes do you? I spent the entirety of the train ride cooped up in the supply car with a hundred sacks of flour and could smell it the entire way here. It gave me a powerful craving for a tall stack of flapjacks."

"The hotel can serve you a breakfast and give you a room," Annabel said, "Roy Mattingly, the husband of the woman you were winking at, owns and runs it. He'll give you a fair price and a soft bed. We don't see many guests outside of hunting season, and that doesn't get started until the snow really starts falling. And be gentle if the subject of Rosanna comes up. Roy and Sarah have looked after her for a bit after her folks left town, and sometimes Mrs. Mattingly can get awfully sensitive on the subject."

"Much obliged for the advice," the marshal grinned, "Let's say we meet at *The Rye in the Sky* at a more civilized hour. How about noon? They serve lunch there I'd hope."

Nodding and wearing a mask of frustration, Annabel mumbled yes. How the man could be thinking about lunch before having his breakfast was beyond her.

"Wonderful. I'll get everything situated with my steed here, and we'll meet in two hours' time. Until then, Sheriff," he said, turning his horse around Annabel to ride into the stable. She heard Mr. Davis complimenting his horse as the marshal dismounted.

10

Annabel stabled her horse and retired to her office to catch a few hours of sleep before having to weather the marshal's odd rambling again. She hoped to heaven he was a quiet drunk, or this afternoon could be a nightmare.

Chapter II

Annabel awoke in her office and stretched out with a yawn as she checked her pocket watch. A quarter to twelve, and almost time to meet the marshal at the saloon. She stretched out on the bed she had slept in, the one in the cell at her office, and pulled her boots on in a daze. She was reluctant to get out of bed, where it had been warm and quiet. The nights were getting colder and colder now, and her old stove did little to stave off the biting winter chill that was quickly approaching the valley.

Her office was a cluttered collection of her life, stored together in the small space for years. A heavy wooden desk was covered with scattered papers, old cartridges from spent bullets, and various books and stationery thrown about with wanton abandon. A few tall cabinets leaned against the walls, with drawers overflowing with yet more papers and clothes. Behind the desk was an unused trunk piled with furs, blankets. Beside it was a large and squat black iron stove rested half-buried under lumber. Above all hung a massive gun rack, holding two rifles that had seen better days. And across from that was a small holding cell made of banded iron. The office was the epitome of dishevelment.

Making her way over to her small black iron stove, she pulled open the creaking metal door and threw a pair of logs into it and packed in a bit of old cotton and tinder.

She struck a match on her gun cabinet and threw it in with the logs of wood. Turning back towards the desk she used her boot to move the stove door shut. As she did so she took up a tin coffeepot and set about preparing the coffee. Walking out the back door, the sheriff made her way to the water pump and worked it a few times, its red painted handle fighting her until it began to pump cold, clear water. She filled the coffeepot and splashed her face a bit before heading back inside. Placing it onto the stove, she then poured beans from a burlap bag into the box grinder on her desk beside some old papers and wrist irons. Hunching over the grinder like a gargoyle, she turned the crank furiously.

Once ground she poured the unevenly textured bits into a cloth bag and submerged it in the now bubbling coffeepot. Two minutes later the roasted aroma filled the office, and the sheriff poured herself a cup. She wanted time to think, time to herself before having to endure the marshal's company again. Sipping her piping hot coffee, she sighed with contentment as she collected herself.

Rosanna had been a friend when the two of them were younger, although Annabel was older than the girl. For a brief window of time, they were inseparable. Peas in a pod, Old Bill used to say. Annabel got older though and became much more serious when the job of sheriff fell to her. They had both grown apart then, and Annabel always felt like was her fault. She would think every now and again how it would be good to talk with Rosanna, to maybe reconnect, but she never got around to it. Now it seemed like she may never get her chance. The girl's parents had gone away a few years ago, leaving Rosanna behind, who found occasional care from the Mattinglys who ran the local hotel.

She could only hope Rosanna had run off with some boy, and wasn't rotting away somewhere in the dark, dead and alone.

It didn't help to think about such horrible things. She could almost hear Mr. Jeffries, the town physician and her closest confidant in her mind, telling her not to jump to morbid conclusions. She relaxed a bit at the thought of the old man, gently helping to ground her. First things first, she had to at least try to gain an idea of where the girl might have gone. There was no sense in fabricating horrors that may have befallen her before Annabel even had a clue as to the girl's movements over the last few days. She had already questioned the Mattinglys, the girl's on and off caretakers, who hadn't seen her for just over a week. Rosanna was the age where a girl is nearly grown up, and she had a great deal of independence here in the valley. With luck, she had simply grown tired of the quiet humdrum of country living and caught a train somewhere out east. It was more likely than anything else that this was exactly what happened to her.

Finishing her coffee Annabel stalked to the door, buckled on her gun belt and collected her hat, and headed outside into the afternoon sun. The warmth of it brought a lightness to Annabel as she walked the packed dirt road of the town's main street. She liked the cold, and here in the valley when the air was crisp and the sun was gentle, it was nearly perfection for her.

Outside, things had calmed down from the bustle of the early morning. Other than a few locals heading out to Humboldt's Creek to trap for beaver, there were no horses on the streets to speak of. The sky overhead was a marbled ocean of blue corn and white cotton, and the air was crisp and cool. Annabel strode over to *The Rye in the Sky* slowly, taking her time as she surveyed her town.

The marshal was already at the door of the establishment, standing on the porch of the saloon. Compared to the scenery around him, blues and golds and the colors of warm wood, he looked faded and grey like a ghost or a wisp of gun smoke. He contrasted violently with the comforting exterior of the saloon itself most of all. The building's siding was a dark worked wood, with frames and shingles of an even darker hue like the crust of a hearty bread. Faded gold letters on the windows displayed its name and year of founding in a looping script that had been painted on almost a decade ago by a travelling calligrapher that had lost a bet with the saloon's proprietor, one Jonas Abernathy. Annabel could hear the beginnings of a polite argument before her boots touched the porch, between the marshal and Henry Colm, the doorman of the establishment.

"I'm sorry sir, I don't care what badge you're waving, but unless it's the sheriff's you have to leave your weapons at the door," he said in his unsure voice.

The marshal was standing beside the doors with his badge in his hand. A plain metal star set into a ring in the fashion the marshals wore. What Annabel found curious was the writing around the ring, which didn't look like English at all. Before she got a good look at it, the marshal sighed and returned the badge to its home on his vest beneath his jacket.

"Sir, I don't mean to insist so firmly. In fact, I think it makes a man seem pushy and impolite to do so. However, given that I am an agent of the law, and by that same law I am required to carry this iron on my person, I would impress on you that the policy of the marshal's office trumps that of this fine saloon."

"I'm sorry sir, but this *ain't* a marshal's office," the kid retorted, "It is a saloon. And the rule says if you don't surrender your arms, you don't get in."

15

"What's going on here, Colm?" she asked the boy, which made him jump. Henry Colm was just old enough to start drinking in the saloon, and took his job seriously as a custodian for the place under the watchful eye of the owner, Jonas Abernathy.

"Afternoon, Sheriff!" he squeaked, "This man says he's some sort of law and wants to bring his revolver in with him. I told him no."

"I'm glad you're here, actually," the marshal said, still smiling, "I didn't mean to argue with the gentleman here. I'm sure you can clear the whole thing up."

"Yes, I can," Annabel said sternly, "I've got my iron with me and that should be enough for the two of us. Unless you're expecting trouble in the middle of the day, you should have no problem complying with Mr. Colm's request."

At first, the marshal looked like she slapped him in the face. After a moment, he tousled his hair and laughed before unbuckling his belt.

"That is fair enough," he chuckled, "I do admit you have a point, Sheriff. I'm just not used to these quiet frontier towns. A man has to learn when to let his guard down."

He handed his gun belt to Colm, who locked it up in a cabinet behind him with a heavy key. Satisfied with his work, the boy's demeanor became much kinder.

"Thank you, sir," the kid said politely, "I didn't mean to be so cross with you, it's just the policy of the house."

"No harm done, friend," the marshal said, "You do good work, Mr. Colm. Take pride in that."

The boy beamed and looked at Annabel as if to say, *did you hear that?* She rolled her eyes and followed the marshal into the saloon.

Piano played in a lazy ramble and hung in the air. The smell of cigar smoke and floor polish lingered over the smell of rich wood, three spirits fighting for dominance in the spacious interior of the saloon. Round tables were set apart throughout the place, some with guests already sitting at them with plates of sausages and potatoes. The marshal nodded appreciatively, his eyes lingering on the small glasses of amber liquid set beside the plates.

Afternoon light played on the floor, lined in neat rows that snaked in from between the slats of the window shutters. Small gas lamps were affixed to the walls and set on every other table, unlit during the day. The marshal smiled at the sight of it, taking in the sight of the large mirrored bar, with each shelf laden with dozens of bottles of liquor. The entire second shelf held one kind of bottle, the house's own whiskey, and the only thing anyone ever really ordered, other than beer. If Ganndo Valley was known for anything, it was known for its fine rye whiskey.

At the bar itself, three men had taken up nearly the entire space of it, practically obscuring the barkeep Mr. Abernathy from view. Two men sat hunched in old wooden stools, while another stood between them, leaning aggressively on the bar. After the sheriff and the marshal entered, he peered at them with hateful suspicion before turning his attention back to the bartender. Annabel paused.

"Something wrong?" the marshal asked.

"I'm not sure. I don't know that man. The big one standing at the bar."

"Well, if he's not from around here, maybe he's seen or heard something about our missing girl on the trail," the marshal said, "Let's say hello and offer the man a drink."

The marshal sauntered ahead, walking past Old Bill and Leeroy playing chess. He stopped just behind the stranger and cleared his throat.

"Pardon me sir, would you mind if I joined you for a drink and a spot of conversation?"

"Go away, lawman," the man said in a caveman grunt.

The piano carried on as the marshal smiled and adjusted his jacket. Annabel watched, listening from near the door. Something felt off about this stranger.

"Pretty keen eyes you have in the back of your head there, partner," he said, shrugging off the man's dismissive command, "The law make you uncomfortable?"

"Don't push me, tinhorn."

"Alright then," the marshal relaxed, "What about either of you fellows? Fancy a drink?"

"They don't drink with law," the big man said. Annabel took a step closer. Near the bar, Leeroy and Old Bill had stopped moving their pieces. The piano player continued to play.

Both men beside the standing man looked incredibly uncomfortable. One of them had sunk his head down so far it almost disappeared beneath the collar of his jacket.

"I'd hear it from them directly, if it's all the same to you."

The man turned his head like an owl, just a little too far around. Enough to make the sheriff's guts squirm a bit. He pressed his heavy hands on the bar and faced the marshal, standing a head taller than the man. A smile crept across the marshal's face, framed underneath his black mustache.

"You'll hear it from my pistol if you don't get lost," he growled, his face still and red with rage.

"That's a dangerous threat to give to a marshal," the marshal said through gritted teeth. His body tensed up, his stance got a little wider. To Annabel the marshal looked like a mountain lion, crouching down and readying itself to strike.

"Perhaps we continue this conversation outside?" he offered to the giant man, "A saloon should be a place of escape and merriment for civilized company."

In response the stranger pulled his coat aside, revealing a revolver in his waistband.

Chapter III

Standing near the bar in the saloon, the marshal's smile remained on his face, now twisted slightly with a knowing glint in his steely black eyes. The drunk who had revealed the hidden pistol tucked into the front his belt clenched his lips together so tightly every drop of blood evacuated them, leaving it as a colorless slit gouged into his red and pitted face. His greasy hair hung about his face in sickly vine-like strands, and his eyes were yellow and gray.

No one made a sound. The piano died abruptly, and many men at cards or in their lunches tilted their heads at the man. Even the sheriff was speechless, licking her lips nervously. Her legs tensed up, and her eyes narrowed. Both slender hands hung loosely at her sides, dangerously near the iron she still wore. Its muted blue steel and sandalwood polished handle reflecting the lazy sunlight that eked through the windows. The marshal's gun was still with the attendant at the door. Sheriff Annabel found herself wishing she had stood up for him when young Henry Colm asked for it. Instead she played her hand with her treatment of strangers, as she often did. She mistrusted outsiders, and this time it seemed her attitude could cost the marshal his life.

The two men beside the armed man stood to join him, emboldened by his actions. Drunk and tense, the three gentlemen at the bar stood unmoving. Brows knitted together into sharp arrows of hate, and they stank of sweat and liquor. Reeking, surly brutes, the lot of them. The one in the center with the pistol stood a head higher than both of his companions, slightly hunched and misshapen, like some primordial man from a time long before. He was a fearsome stranger to the sheriff, and even from where she stood she could sense the stranger's radiating malice like heat from a furnace. The marshal stood his ground. Steadfast in his resolve, unflinching, with eyes passing slowly from one of them to the next, never resting on the pistol that the center man had smuggled in. His gaze did not betray the slightest measure of fear.

A chair creaked awkwardly, and that was all it took to ignite the fuse.

Spinning like a dancer, the marshal's jacket flared out as he twisted on his bootheel away from the revolver as the drunk pulled leather. Mid-spin, he kicked out at the man's wrist as the pistol fired, throwing the ball into the wooden ceiling amidst a cloud of thick smoke. The crack caused many patrons to scream and flee, and the sheriff drew her own pistol, trying to cry out over the noise.

Jonas Abernathy, the barkeep, flung himself behind the sanctuary of the bar, while the batwing doors swung wildly from patrons stampeding into the street, crying murder.

The drunk on the right, Thomas O'Toole it looked to be, headbutted the marshal and sent the man to the ground, his face aglow with pain. His nose fountained blood onto his black mustache, and his eyes went wild as he fell.

In the center of their group the drunk with the gun wheeled to take aim at the fallen lawman. His face was a malformed grimace

21

of hatred so mad he appeared no longer human. Annabel thumbed back the hammer of her weapon and shot him. His chest exploded and threw blood across the barroom floor as he was thrown back like a scarecrow onto the bar. Glasses were knocked aside and smashed, and whiskey flowed with blood onto the floorboards.

The two unarmed men froze at the sound of her shot, both rooted to the spot. One greedily eyed his fallen comrade's pistol, his face a Neanderthal mixture of fear and anger.

"You try for it, and you're a dead man," Annabel said with her jaw screwed shut with purpose. O'Toole didn't move.

Groaning and getting to his feet, the marshal produced a kerchief from his pocket and dabbed at his trickling nose, wiping away the fresh blood that had begun to run from his nostrils.

A snap from the batwing doors announced the arrival of Mr. Jeffries, who stopped dead at the sight of the saloon.

"Good heavens!" he cried, raising a trembling hand to his mouth. Annabel looked to the doctor with a creeping sense of regret. Of everyone in town, he was the last person she would have wanted to see this. Mr. Jeffries had been like a father to her, and now here she was standing before him with a smoking gun in hand, mere paces away from the corpse of a man she had just killed.

"It's alright, Mr. Jeffries," the sheriff said.

The marshal laughed, sniffing painfully and wincing with a rough grin, "I'd wager your sheriff is correct. I don't expect any further commotion from these gentlemen here," he gestured to the two men at the bar, who appeared to be sobering up rather quickly.

Taking a careful step towards the fallen man, the marshal knelt and retrieved the dead man's gun, and placed it into his pocket.

Neither of the other two strangers at the counter made a move to stop him, both still eyed the sheriff wearily.

Sheriff Annabel felt her shoulders relaxing. She kept her iron pointed at the two, its hammer still raised like a rattler's tail.

By the door, Henry Colm rose from behind his counter, shaking so badly it made his keyring jangle and chitter with ringing metallic tones. Colm gulped and looked from the sheriff to the marshal, and then at the ragged mess of a man sprawled dead upon the floor. The marshal looked up from the dead man and gestured to the two men beside him.

"Unless you've managed to conceal irons on your person, Sheriff, I suggest you escort these two rabble-rousers to the jailhouse," the marshal said with one eyebrow cocked, his swagger returning almost immediately, despite the fact that blood continued to trickle from his nostrils.

Annabel blinked hard and snorted.

"I don't need you telling me how to run my office," she growled, gesturing with her free hand to the men at the bar, "You two, come with me. I caution you to walk very slowly. If you move in a sudden manner, I'll put a bullet in you."

The two stepped carefully around the pooling mess that was their companion and were led out by the sheriff, who gave one last, hard look at the marshal as she did so.

He raised his black and heavy eyebrows and exhaled sharply, again wincing. Coughing once, he straightened up and adjusted the lapels of his jacket.

"I believe she may shoot those two in the back whether they have the initiative to run or not, Mr. Jeffries. Your Sheriff certainly has a venomous temperament."

The old doctor adjusted his glasses clumsily, still a bit shaken.

"You just have to get to know her, marshal," he croaked, still reeling from the sight of the dead man, "she's the truest soul I have ever known. I practically raised that girl, and I'd doubt you'd find anyone with that kind of grit from here to Mantis City."

The marshal chuckled to himself and smirked as he nodded in agreement. Creaking and thumping, the floor protested at every footfall as the marshal approached the attendant near the door.

"Mr. Colm was it?" he asked. The man behind the counter nodded, "Since there are no patrons left for me to menace with my weapon, do you suppose I could get my pistol back?"

The thin man stared at the marshal with bulbous and unblinking eyes. He neither moved nor reacted, leaving the man's revolver where it was.

Grinning and shaking his head, the marshal stepped away.

"I suppose it'll be there when we leave, anyhow. You can hold it for me until such time when Mr. Jeffries and I are finished here," he said, walking back over to the body of the dead man. The barkeep had donned his jacket and was making a hasty exit when the marshal stopped him, placing a hand firmly on the man's shoulder.

"Hold on there, friend. I'd like to field a question to you. How much for a glass of that whiskey?"

"A…a what?" he asked.

"A glass of whiskey. Unless I am mistaken, you folks make your own whiskey in these parts, and I've heard tell in Tecumac that it's one of the finest spirits a man can enjoy. I often fancy a fine drink during contemplation, and I do intend on doing some contemplating with the good doctor here for a bit."

Struck mute by the strangeness of the question, the barman could only work his lips open and closed for a moment. The marshal produced a dollar from his billfold and neatly placed it into the barman's jacket pocket, giving it two pats after it was placed.

"I suspect that will do finely for a few glasses here. We'll tidy up the saloon, friend. I thank you for the drink."

With a heavy clap on the barman's back, the marshal gently herded him out past Mr. Jeffries and Mr. Colm. The attendant began to leave as well before the marshal stopped him.

"Now son, I can't let you leave your cage of firearms there unmonitored. I'm afraid you'll have to stay, but I can afford you a glass of whiskey if you'd like."

The kid nodded slowly, still processing the scene. The cloud of gunpowder hadn't yet had time to properly dissipate and hung about the ceiling like a profane storm waiting to break.

"Mr. Jeffries, whiskey?" the marshal asked, sauntering to the bar and stepping around the expired drunk on the floor, careful not to get any blood on the soles of his boots.

"I don't take whiskey..." he said weakly, still processing the scene as if it were a nightmare he would shortly wake from, "Brandy will do for me," he added automatically.

The marshal set his bloodied kerchief on the bar and selected the brandy first, pouring the deep amber-colored liquid into a glass, before corking it and fetching the whiskey for himself.

As he poured the whiskey for himself and Mr. Colm, the marshal snorted a bit and spat blood into the spittoon beside the bar. It smacked quietly into the brass and the marshal sucked his teeth disappointment.

"I never could figure how to get it to ring proper," he muttered, ferrying the brandy to Mr. Jeffries and the whiskey to Mr. Colm, "But now, we must retain our focus on the matter at hand. Doctor, I'd like your assistance with our friend by the bar here."

Barely gripping his brandy, the doctor looked from the body to the marshal in confusion.

"Marshal, this man is dead."

"And?"

"And?! Well…I mean. He's *dead*, marshal," Mr. Jeffries sputtered into his brandy, "I can't do anything for him now, perforated as he is."

"I'd like you to assist me in examining him, as it were," the marshal said, drinking his whiskey and freezing in place. Eyes wide and mouth agape, he stared at the remaining contents of his glass, "That is a *fine* whiskey indeed!" he exclaimed breathlessly. "Damn fine, if you'll pardon my profanity."

With a last, long pull from the glass he emptied it at once and sighed contentedly.

"You want me to examine him?" Mr. Jeffries asked, approaching the dead man with his brandy glass clasped in both hands.

"Precisely, Mr. Jeffries. I'd like your assistance in determining the cause of death."

Mr. Jeffries said nothing, regarding the dead man with confusion, eyes drawn to the hole in his chest where the sheriff's ball had struck him. The marshal poured himself another whiskey, leaned his back against the bar, and sniffled a bit.

"Mister weren't he shot?" the young attendant squeaked by the door, his whiskey untouched.

"Very astute, Mr. Colm. The gunshot is what killed him. I am more interested in learning the *cause* of death."

"Ain't that the same thing?" the boy asked. The marshal laughed.

"It can be, though in this case I very much doubt that. Why draw on the law, stranger or otherwise, with the town sheriff present? Why smuggle the gun into the establishment in the first place? And more importantly, how did he know who I was and why I was here?"

Both men the marshal queried were silent for a moment.

"He did know you was a marshal, even before you said anything to him," young Mr. Colm acknowledged.

"And what's more," the marshal added, pointing to the dead man, "He attempted to kill me in front of more than twenty witnesses and the Sheriff. Supposing he succeeded, he'd surely be hanged for murder. What could make this man take such a risk, I wonder?"

"Men do mad things when deep in drink, friend," Mr. Jeffries explained, speaking plainly, "I do not know this man, but I know his friends, Mr. O'Toole and Mr. Dweyer. Both are prone to drink and vice, and sometimes become violent. Nothing like this, of course," he knelt beside the deceased patron, "Once O'Toole unhorsed himself trying to skip fences. Swore it was the drover what sold the horse to him lame and set about striking the man with a poker. Spent the weekend in the jailhouse."

"Do you know him, Mr. Colm?" the marshal asked. The boy shook his head.

"Well then, let's get a measure of the man. Mr. Jeffries, what do you make of this?" the marshal asked, crouching alongside the doctor near the dead man.

Propping him up to a sitting position, the marshal set the back of the dead man's head against the bar. He took his thumb and forefinger and pried the man's mouth open, worming his fingers against the corpse's gums to work them away from the man's teeth.

Mr. Jeffries gasped in revulsion. A stink like tar and pitch emanated from the dead man's mouth. His teeth were thin and horribly discolored, yellowed bone set into his gums. Worst of all were the man's slick and oozing gums themselves, which were the bruised black and purple color of a rotted plum. Metallic black slime coated the teeth and tongue as the marshal examined the corpse.

The marshal grimaced, and his eyes narrowed. His expression became fearsome, and he stood rapidly, removing his fingers from the corpse's mouth. He poured what remained of his second whiskey over them and wiped them on his slacks.

"Have you ever seen a substance or an illness that can do something like that, Mr. Jeffries?"

Mr. Jeffries could only stare at the body. They had not even taken the time to close its eyes, and it felt almost as if the dead man were staring back at him.

Chapter IV

"Get a move on fellas, and no dallying on the porch," Sheriff Annabel snapped, shoving Mr. O'Toole up the creaking step of the Sheriff's Office porch. Mr. Dweyer did not need any extra urging and plodded forward on his own. Out of the two, Dweyer seemed more possessed and preoccupied with his guilt, while O'Toole looked resentful and dangerous now that he had been caught.

O'Toole opened the door, his shaggy head hanging in defeat and the sheriff led him and Dweyer at gunpoint into the lockup.

Both stepped into the large cell and Annabel shut the door behind them and locked it with a crank of the heavy iron key. She leaned in towards the men with her hand still on the handle of her holstered revolver, glaring hellfire at them to assert her authority.

"You both stew a bit while I try to muster what I can charge you with," she fell into her old wooden chair and rubbed her temples and her face. A dead man on the floor of the *Rye*. This marshal had been in town for less than a day and already there had been a shootout at the saloon. After so many years of relative quiet out here in town, thunder and chaos seemed to have fallen upon the valley all at once.

It was overwhelming, and Annabel could not help but feel trapped under a deluge of misfortune as she re-loaded her pistol at her desk. The disappearance of that girl, the cattle from Williamson's farm, and now she had shot a man at the *Rye in the Sky*.

She swore to herself, leaping up from her chair and stomping out the back door of the office with her fists clenched tightly, startling both of her prisoners.

What a colossally stupid idea, allowing the post to go out running that story mentioning that missing girl. She could have stopped it, should have known the feds would try to interfere and now...now she had killed a man in front of everyone at the *Rye*.

She had shot people before. A few outlaws looking to skip bail in July had tried to steal a few colts from the Colm's, and as they fled and fired upon her and Henry's father, Annabel had shot them both dead, earning young Henry's admiration and respect. Even with the absence of his father, and with Mr. Abernathy at the saloon looking after him, he treated her differently after seeing that kill. She had built a reputation with the kid, and by his telling of the tale she had a reputation with the town. But she had never gunned down a man like that, and never dreamed of doing it so close to home. Where she drank and laughed and went in at cards with friends and neighbors. Now, she knew, they would forever think of her as a killer, looking at her like Henry did. She wondered if any of them could ever look at her again without seeing her shoot that man in cold blood in their mind's eye.

Swirling in her mind as a crimson tide, she could see his chest explode, blood and bone erupting forth in waves tall enough to capsize the world. An unnatural amount of blood, so much to be trapped in such a small, comfortable place. It would leave stains that could never truly be washed away in her heart. For a moment she wondered if she was wrong to have shot the man.

"No," she said to herself, staring down at the cold grey-brown ground, her mouth issuing steam like a dragon, "Don't do that," she commanded herself. There was no use in denying that had she hesitated, that man would have fired upon the saloon.

That drifter would have killed the marshal a second later if she had faltered. The choice was out of her hands. Why did the buffoon still try to draw down on the marshal? He'd still be alive if it weren't for that mad look of murder in his eyes, guiding his hand to point that pistol down at the marshal with the intent to kill.

No sane man, drunk or not, would take that chance. If anything, it would have made more sense for him to shoot at her than the marshal.

It felt disgusting to think it, but Annabel was relieved the man was a stranger. She certainly didn't know him, and with how often Dweyer and O'Toole rode out into the sticks it wouldn't surprise her if he was just a nobody. A drifter or criminal. Maybe he was completely mad.

Either way, she intended to find out exactly what happened back there at the saloon. Strangers were rarely in town for more than a day or two at most, and they never made much noise. Not one of them had tried anything so mad as what happened today. Taking a few deep breaths, she began to calm down. And as soon her hands were steady enough to rustle around in her poke, she rolled a cigarette, which she popped between her lips before heading back inside.

She whipped the door open and watched the men in the cell jump as it slammed into the wall behind it. She stepped up to the cage glaring like a mad dog.

31

"If the devil hasn't sobered you up yet you had best hope he does so now," she growled quietly, gripping the unlit cigarette tightly between her teeth. Both men in the cell remained quiet, with Dweyer looking as if he feared Annabel would shoot him at a moment's notice. O'Toole appeared cruel and withdrawn.

"I am a tinker's cuss away from just leading you out into the woods and shooting you both for bringing that violence into my town. If you frustrate me in the slightest in the next few moments, I will strip you down, bind your hands, and drag you into the pines to die without a bullet. Do you understand me?"

The two drunks stared with glassy and bloodshot eyes. Dweyer began to weep silently, tears running down his face freely. O'Toole licked his lips over and over and appeared as though he was struggling to breathe. He looked like a man in fits.

"Well that doesn't sound too hospitable of a thing to say to your prisoners," said a voice by the door. Annabel turned in a flash and drew her pistol only to be facing the marshal, leaning against the office wall with his hat tucked under one arm. The other was holding a glass from the *Rye in the Sky*, filled to the brim with whiskey.

"Damn it, marshal, I could have shot you," she hissed, holstering her weapon. The marshal shrugged.

"Which would *also* not be very hospitable. Or lawful, if we're speaking plain," he said, walking over to her setting his glass on the heavy desk. With a careful motion, he placed his hat neatly beside it and brushed some dust from the brim of it. He sat down in her chair and leaned back while she glared at him with a gaze full of hellfire.

"Sheriff, I'd like to have a moment to question your prisoners, if you don't mind," he said lazily, while rocking obnoxiously in her chair, which creaked and squeaked in protest.

"I *do* mind," she said, reigning in her frustration, "I can question them myself, and I'd like to start by finding the name of the man I just killed, and why he tried to shoot a federal marshal in broad daylight in front of me."

"And you're in my chair," she added, with a hint of malice returning to her voice.

The marshal didn't get up, but he did stop rocking. He locked eyes with Annabel and for a moment she felt a slight twinge of discomfort. She felt immediately aware of how savagely she was behaving. Shame and embarrassment welled up in her gut. The marshal nodded politely and stood up, setting his hat atop the rack behind the desk.

"I'm sure you gentlemen aren't feeling particularly happy about your current circumstances, are you?" he asked politely, sitting at the empty chair across the desk facing the prisoners.

"Naw, sir. We ain't happy with our circumstance," O'Toole said, gulping down his fear.

"Mr. O'Toole, I presume?" the marshal asked, producing a small pencil and notebook from his jacket. The man nodded. His face was awash with a film of sweat, and he reeked of liquor that seemed so potent Annabel wondered how he was still conscious.

"My condolences to you and your compadre, Mr. Dweyer, for the loss of your yet-to-be-identified companion. Assuming you three were on friendly terms, I mean."

The marshal scribbled in his notebook, and Annabel couldn't make out what he was writing. After a bit of silence, he stopped.

"Gentleman," he said in a very measured and careful tone, "Did the man say anything to you before the violence started, either before or after he threatened your lives with his reckless actions?"

Sheriff Annabel flicked her eyes from the marshal to the two thugs in the cage. Dweyer froze with his mouth agape while O'Toole continued to sweat and squirm.

Both prisoners froze like lizards caught in the open, trying to look inconspicuous while also trying to think of a way to bolt out and run.

The marshal set his notebook and pencil in his pocket, then leaned forward and made a steeple with his fingertips.

"You seemed as thick as thieves, pardon," he said, stopping himself, "As thick as *alleged* thieves, back at that saloon. Surely you knew the man's name, correct? A kindred spirit met on the trail, perhaps? If the Sheriff can have that, you can leave."

Annabel was too awestruck at the reaction of the men in the cell to shout or contradict the marshal, and simply watched him speak.

"The thing is," the marshal said, "I don't think you actually *do* know his name. Mr. Jeffries and I took a quick inventory of the aftermath of our fracas, and oddly enough I only found two glasses where the three of you were sitting. And considering that you are both sweating booze right now, I'm fairly certain that your pal wasn't drinking with you."

"What was also curious, is that he had been standing between the two of you when I entered with Sheriff Annabel here. You were both seated at stools in front of the bar. Two stools, with the dead man standing between them, without a seat of his own. So why weren't you all seated together? There were plenty of open stools for you all to have sat together enjoying that miraculous whiskey, yet he was wedged between you. Like he had forced himself in."

Mr. Dweyer had begun to cry again, his eyes soundlessly leaking, spilling tears down his shaking cheeks.

The marshal's face became sincerely sympathetic. Annabel caught herself believing he might actually care for the fates of these men, while also uncertain at the same time about his sincerity.

"There's no need to cry, Mr. Dweyer. The man is dead, and you are both safe here in the Sheriff's office. Safest place in town, I'd wager. She's clearly a crack-shot and reacts fast enough. Not a minute ago she almost shot me," he laughed, "The dead man can't hurt you now."

"Sure he can," Mr. Dweyer blubbered quietly. Annabel and the marshal stared at him intently. The wind outside whistled as he said it, hauntingly quiet, like a whisper itself.

"Why would you think that, Amos?" Annabel asked, walking closer to the cage.

"Don't you make a mess of it now," O'Toole said, his fear and sorrow making way for ferocity.

"He'll come up and drink our breath, he'll sing the dirge that eats men's souls," Dweyer wailed, screaming and hysterical now, his hands flying up to the side of his head.

The marshal stood slowly, rising from his chair with his eyes locked on Mr. Dweyer, who had begun to scream as O'Toole shouted obscenities at him. O'Toole was babbling and becoming more and more enraged, now standing over Dweyer, who was

35

backed into the corner of the cell. Cascading out of his mouth were words that sounded like another language to the sheriff. Harsh, guttural sounds almost like an animal.

"Sheriff get that door open," the marshal said coolly over the men's ranting.

Annabel fumbled with her keys, and all at once O'Toole fell upon Dweyer with violence. Both men were wordlessly screaming and gurgling amidst the sounds of blows, entangled together in the cage. The marshal could see blood.

"Now Anna!" the marshal yelled, and Annabel dropped the keys.

Without a word, the marshal drew his revolver and shot O'Toole twice in the back, and fired a third round at the lock, blasting it open in a storm of smoke and noise, before he yanked the door open and entered the cell.

Mr. O'Toole lay dead atop Mr. Dweyer. The marshal pulled the heavy man aside with a grunt and hissed when he saw Dweyer.

The man was twitching slightly, his shirt was bibbed with blood. O'Toole had torn at the man's throat with his teeth. Mr. Dweyer sputtered and seized, eyes rolling back in his head in his suffering.

The marshal flicked back the hammer of his revolver and shot him in the head.

Annabel stooped to retrieve the keys, her body moving on its own, and she tried to work the ruined lock as if the cell weren't already open. Her movements were frantic and erratic, and she was breathing raggedly, unable to confront the nature of what had just transpired. Holstering his still-smoking iron, the marshal spoke gently to the sheriff.

"Sheriff, it's done with. You can stop that now," the marshal said, trying to place a hand on her arm. She fought against his touch, and began to sob with eyes full of fear, sorrow, and hate. She wailed and screamed at the marshal, pointing a shaking finger at the bodies in the cage.

"What is happening? What is *happening*?! What have you done to these people?!"

His face twisted in pity, the marshal said nothing, instead electing to stoop down to recover the unlit cigarette that she had dropped. He drew a match from his trouser pocket and lit the cigarette, before passing it back to the sheriff.

She took a few long drags before her limbs became as jelly, and she had to steady herself on her desk. Blood had begun to pool in the cell and was running out onto the floor and near the ugly rug by the door. The marshal picked it up and set it safely atop a cabinet.

Without turning to face her, he exhaled deeply.

"I'm sorry," he said, speaking oddly, searching for the right words, "I am truly sorry that such misfortune has befallen this beautiful and secluded place. When my department saw the letter from here, the report by mail, whispers began to circulate about a case we worked out here a long time ago. I spent about a week in the stacks looking over what was left of the old case files. I rode out hoping it wasn't true. Hoping they were wrong."

Stepping through the shallow puddle of blood, he returned to the chair opposite the sheriff, and took up his whiskey again, studying it.

"We don't know what it is for sure. Sometimes I genuinely believe despite all of our miracles and marvelous advancements we really don't know spit about anything. There was something here a long time ago in Ganndo Valley, preying upon the travelers and first settlers here. Reportedly, we stopped it back then. Yet here it is again, wearing the skins of men sipping your fine whiskey with a monster tearing up their insides."

"That's impossible," Annabel whispered, "People come and go all the time. That's all it is. People come and go."

"Look me in the eye and tell me that's what you really think is happening. Tell me how well you know those two disfigured masses in your cell behind you. Something is *feeding* on your town, Sheriff."

"*You are insane*," Annabel growled with a smoldering venom on her lips, her cigarette a flickering stub hanging from her lips, "If you think for one second you know more about my people and *my town* than I do, you're a lunatic. There's no such thing that can do what you say, and there is no sinister backroom reason why folks don't stay here."

"Sheriff," the marshal said quietly as he raised his hand, "How often have strangers come through only to never be seen again? Men and women who drift don't leave much of a trail behind them, but after putting the pieces together the disappearances go back a long way. Can you tell me how many people have left town without saying goodbye? How is it that with such a beautiful and idyllic town, no one new decides to settle here?"

"There's no such thing..." she murmured. A slow and viscous reality began to set in as she spoke, her rage and disbelief gave way to sorrow and naked fear. The cigarette butt fell from her now trembling lips and her fists unclenched. In a moment, her entire body relaxed in defeat and she stared at the ceiling to keep herself steady. The marshal laid his hand on her shoulder carefully.

"Sheriff, I need your help with this. Your point about you knowing this place is true. I need you."

He held out his hand holding the clean glass of whiskey towards her. Green and glittering halfway between terror and rage, her eyes stared back at the still amber liquid within.

"I don't know if I have the strength," she whispered. The marshal said nothing, "What if I say no? I tell you to take your lunacy far away from the valley, then what?"

"Then I do my best alone, Sheriff. I have no choice," he replied, shrugging while still holding the offered drink out towards her, "I go and check on the movements of the dead men and try to retrace their path over the last few days."

"I'm not going to let you walk around my town talking about this. Rosanna and her family are good people. What am I supposed to tell them? A monster or a demon took their little girl?" she snapped, stepping nearer to the stranger now. She was so close to him she could smell the blood and whiskey on his mustache.

"You won't have to tell them anything. They never made it to Rue Gri. In fact, no one has seen or heard from them for almost a year. It's taken them too, Annabel. It's devouring your town."

All motion was stolen from her at the words. In his black eyes she could see a distorted reflection of herself standing there, stiff with anger, with a silver badge glimmering on her chest. If she hoped to honor that star she wore, in spite of her own fears and doubts, she had to act. To do anything less would be an affront to everything her belief in the law stood for. Dweyer and O'Toole were her only leads, the last people to be seen with Rosanna. Even if the marshal was crazy, he was right. They needed each other.

"I'll help you then," she said while backing away from the man in gray, "But I want to be clear that I don't believe for a second that there's some weird hocus pocus going on with these men. They drank a bad batch of moonshine or took too much opium in my opinion and that's the last we'll speak of it, agreed?"

The marshal nodded with an expression that agreed with a part of what she said.

"We're concentrating on finding the missing girl, Rosanna. If these men were involved with her disappearance as we suspected, she may be in danger. With luck, we can find her together, and if not, with the further support of the marshal's office. We can talk to the townsfolk, see who last spoke with any of the three dead men."

The marshal sighed, drinking the whiskey himself, slowly. He examined the empty glass carefully before gently setting it down, then locking eyes with Annabel.

"You're a good woman, Sheriff. And a fine officer of the law. I find your terms agreeable and will do my best to refrain from voicing my opinions on the subject. For now."

Quietly, the man stepped over to retrieve his hat from the rack behind the desk and placed it atop his head. Annabel saw him lick his lips thoughtfully, as if he were about to say something, before he shook his head and cleared his throat, as if he had changed his mind as to what he was going to say.

"I'll check with Mr. Jeffries and see about removing these poor souls from your office before they soil it any further. Opium or not, they'll be leaving a powerful smell all too soon."

Annabel nodded. The blood from both of them had oozed from the cell and now almost reached the cabinets on the opposite wall.

"I'll see you tomorrow, then," she said, trying not to look at the ruin of her prisoners. The marshal smiled the slightest bit and tipped his hat to her.

"For what the opinion of an old peacock is worth, you are very brave Sheriff Annabel."

At that, he left, striding through the creaking door and leaving her alone for a moment. Turning in knots, her stomach tried to make sense of her conflicting mistrust of the marshal, and the fact that the same feelings almost killed the man earlier.

Leaving the office behind, she stepped out into the street which felt different. Changed somehow by what had transpired that day. Despite what darkness had fallen on the valley today, she could not shake the biting fear at the back of her neck, whispering in wicked tones that the worst was yet to come.

Chapter V

Soft edged and silent, the breeze slithered over the grasses outside of Ganndo Valley, moving the emerald blades in concert as massive waves.

Annabel had retired to her ranch after the horrors of the day before. Knowing that two bodies were left in the cell overnight made her stomach turn in knots, but she could not bear the thought of asking poor Mr. Jeffries to prepare two further coffins for the mangled souls within that iron cage. Fingers cold with fear pulled at her keyring, and she placed the tiny brass thing into the lock of the office door and opened it. With a small gasp, she almost dropped the keys.

The bodies were gone.

No sign was left of either Dweyer or O'Toole, and aside from the planks of the cell floor being a bit more washed out and faded in color, it appeared as though nothing at all had happened.

What's more, she was not alone in the sheriff's office. In her chair once again was the marshal, sipping coffee straight from a tall tin carafe. Steam wreathed his head like a congregation of specters, and he grinned and raised it at Annabel as one would raise a toast.

"Good morning Sheriff. I suppose it's too much to hope you rested well after the misfortune authored here last night."

"I slept just fine," she said sternly, placing her hat onto the rack firmly enough to make it wobble in place.

"Ah," the marshal remarked, satisfied. He took another gulp from the carafe and loudly sighed with satisfaction. The sheriff crossed her arms and her eyes narrowed.

"The chair."

"Oh, right!" the marshal said as he hopped to his feet and brushed the seat of the chair with the back of his hand, "Apologies, Sheriff."

Annabel did not sit down, rather she leaned against the heavy wooden desk and adjusted her belt.

"You moved them," she remarked while looking over the cell again, empty and quiet. Shadows played across the iron bars that fell upon the cleaned planks of the floor.

"Mr. Jeffries and I, yes," the marshal said, "Early this morning, I asked him for lye to do the deed and he commenced to insist that he help supervise. I don't think he trusted me with the chemicals to be truthful with you."

"You used *lye*?"

"Only way to be certain that we get everything. Don't want anything listening in on us in your office. I'll leave it at that, since I did agree to your terms on discussing what happened to these men."

Her words were pressure building in the locomotive of her heart, bursting to get free and verbally assault the foreign lawman for even mentioning it again. In a moment she took a deep breath

43

and relaxed, her hands automatically moving to her tobacco poke. The marshal stroked his mustache pensively.

"Given that our one lead is dead, our best course of action would be to examine the late gentlemen before they are laid to their final rest."

The sheriff inhaled the wrong way mid-pull on her cigarette and fell into a coughing fit. Waiting patiently, the marshal said nothing and made no move to interrupt her.

"Examine them for *what?*" she wheezed, pounding her chest with a clenched fist. The marshal started to move towards her for help, and the sheriff's hand shot up with the speed of a striking rattler to halt him. He pretended to have moved to brush off his vest with his hands and adjusted his shirt collar.

"For details on their activities, of course. One can learn a lot from the dead in a sense."

"So, you can speak with the dead now, is that it?" she quipped mockingly. Instead of looking insulted, the marshal grinned in a way that made Annabel apprehensive and slightly disturbed.

"In a way, Sheriff, the dead have ways of communicating certain truths to the living. Truths they sometimes cannot trust when *spoken* by the living. Let's take a walk to Mr. Jeffries, and I'll give you a language lesson you'll not soon forget."

Out in the pleasant and cradling warmth of the spring sunshine, the town was alive with activity.

The valley was small, even for a frontier town, but many who came to the northwest during the silver rush in search for riches found riches of another sort in the valley. People found a peace and contentment most can only dream of, and folks who remained after the speculators left lived good lives out on the frontier. What few mines were laid after stakes were claimed yielded ore of poor quality in pitiful quantities. A pair of speculators from out east had come and taken an appraisal of the mine, only to sadly declare it would be more expensive to finish setting up operations than to abandon them altogether. The rail did not make it far enough north to help the town along in those days, and it grew slowly and comfortably over time. The land was good for grazing and a little growing, and the many crystal-clear streams and lakes of cool water made for excellent fishing and hunting. A great forest of pines bordered the town on the north side and was wondrous to behold. Thousands of trees stood as iron green fanged spires that stretched for miles and miles. The forest was so vast it reached all the way to the mountains that one could see in the distance on days when the sky was clear. The sky was thankfully clear quite often in Ganndo Valley, and at night when the world was blanketed with stars it was a magical place.

Currently in the morning light it was also a comforting sight for the sheriff. Wagons and coaches were pulled along by all manner of horses, and many people were out to shop or work. The red-striped pole outside the barber shop spun lazily, advertising five cent haircuts and three cent shaves. Across the street candy glimmered invitingly in the window in enormous jars stuffed with candies in a rainbow of tantalizing colors at the general store. Bunting hung from porches and balconies, and piano played in ragtime hung in the air from the saloon, already recovered from

45

the terrors that had happened there the day before. Across the street a boy swept the porch of the town's church, a small white building with a grey spire and two beautiful stained-glass windows.

Like a child the marshal whistled, and his focus jumped from one thing to the next as they walked together.

More than a few of the people out and about looked as if they were still half asleep, walking slowly and clumsily, avoiding the marshal. Annabel guessed that perhaps the news of the commotion at the saloon made them weary of the marshal, but there was something more to it. They seemed almost preoccupied with something else, something so profound it made it difficult to concentrate even on walking around.

Other than those few who seemed out of sorts, many townsfolk happily greeted Annabel and her strange escort as the pair passed through the streets, tipping hats or giving waves. Mrs. Mattingly practically winked at the marshal as she left the general store, carrying an enormous flour sack over one shoulder. Annabel responded to each of these with a slight nod and a careful smile.

"Tight-knit community around here, Sheriff. It's a beautiful thing to see, really."

"The valley is small," she replied, "Everyone has to do their part to keep this great wheel named civilization turning. After rich folks out east realized the mine was a dud, they halted progress on the rail coming here. Families who had set down and built homes and businesses out here were stranded and had to make do. I'm only sheriff because we had to make do."

"That's a sad and frankly incorrect assumption in my opinion," the man with the mustache interjected, seeing the light fade from Annabel's face as she made her depressing declaration, "From

46

what I've seen so far these people think very highly of you, and on my personal account you're top-notch law. Certainly, worthy for a beautiful place like this. A place worth protecting. Worth saving."

He finished as they came to a stop in front of the doctor's office, smiling at her reassuringly. She spat in the dirt and shook her head, smiling in satisfaction despite herself.

"One more thing," she said. "Be gentle with Mr. Jeffries. He's tough enough for frontier living but I don't need you carrying on about monsters with the man. Ghost stories eat at him even when told during daylight hours."

"You know this fellow pretty well then I take it?" the marshal asked. Annabel shrugged.

"I've known him all my life," Annabel said quietly. Mr. Jeffries was the only soul in the valley that Annabel felt she could truly be herself around. Her badge influenced her manner in almost everything, except with old Mr. Jeffries. Having coffee with him on Sundays kept her grounded, and when they sat down to talk all the walls came tumbling down for her. She could tell him anything. In many ways he was much like a father to her, and it was no secret to anyone that after Mr. Jeffries looked after Annabel as if she were his own daughter.

Pine needles were as green embers carried on the breath of a quiet wind before them. Near the doctor's the foot traffic was quieter and solemn. Beside his large flat board building was another office with no name that displayed its wares made of pine board on the porch. The proprietor of the neighboring business sat on the railings of said porch, gently strumming a guitar missing a string and nodding to the pair of law. He sized up the marshal almost immediately and caused the stranger's smile to fade just a little.

"Men who take too much pleasure in that profession have always made my flesh jitter," the marshal said to the sheriff just loudly enough so the man with the guitar could hear him, before holding open the door for her to enter the office of the doctor, Mr. Jeffries. A small brass bell rang on its hook as the door swung casually open.

A single room awaited them beyond the threshold, displaying tables and shelves arrayed neatly. Clean linens topped the examination tables, and a few instruments and tools were polished and set away in jars of alcohol along the shelves. Glimmering on a desk near the back of the room were lollipops in an open-topped jar. Mr. Jeffries had been sitting at the desk writing when the sheriff entered, and he rose at the sound of the door's bell.

"Howdy Sheriff, and howdy to you sir," he said grinning, his spectacles awkwardly sliding down his nose before he adjusted them with a firm tug on their arms.

"Morning, Mr. Jeffries," Annabel said, removing her hat, "The marshal has an odd request for you, and asked I accompany him. It's about Rosanna."

The doctor's face was a winter moon atop a coat of white.

"Oh, that business again. I feel dreadful just thinking of it," he said, steadying himself on his desk, "And a strange request from the marshal, you say? Pardon my saying marshal, but the only *sensible* request you've made since you arrived here in town was to ask for whiskey at the saloon."

The marshal shrugged and approached the old doctor.

"Sir, I don't suppose you've delivered the departed men to the grim gentleman next door yet, have you?"

"No, sir," Jeffries responded with suspicion, "Both of them are back in the private room. The stranger Annabel shot, pardon ma'am," he added nervously, as if he were afraid of offending her. She twirled her finger in the air for him to continue, "The stranger's already been delivered to the undertaker."

"I'd like to see them, if you please."

Dumbfounded at the request, the physician could only stare. He puttered for a moment, his mind racing to make sense of the thing before he took a deep breath and idly grabbed a lollipop from the jar.

"But marshal, *why?* Good lord, you've seen both men just this morning, what else could you possibly hope to learn from another round of macabre poking and prodding of the dead? You've already examined their teeth quite gruesomely back at the sheriff's like some shifty drover and now, now you…"

Patient and calm, the marshal waited until the doctor's rant slowly wound down. His face looked gentle and calming to Annabel, like that of a parent watching a child in the throes of a tantrum or fit.

"Mr. Jeffries, I wouldn't ask if I didn't honestly believe it could be some help in our search to find young Miss Rosanna. I do not plan on any sort of desecration to these men. You'll find them exactly how they are now when my business is concluded."

The doctor popped the candy into his mouth and wrung his hands, blinking repeatedly and looking at the floor. The man was clearly conflicted with the request by this stranger to further meddle with the dead. It wasn't natural. The way the stranger looked at them, and how he looked at the stranger dead in the saloon reminded Jeffries of how a man would look at a butterfly collection. It was no way to honor or respect the dead. Annabel

49

cleared her throat, and Mr. Jeffries looked to her, standing tall with her hat in her hands.

"Doctor, please. You can take the marshal's word on this. It's our only lead."

Jeffries sighed, and collected himself.

"Alright, Sheriff. But I'm observing as well. These men are in my care until the rites are read and the coffins are laid down, dead or not."

Opening a drawer of the desk, he withdrew a key and led the sheriff and marshal to the back door of the room. He unlocked the door and gestured for them to enter.

The atmosphere of the back room was a reeking miasma of chemicals. The smell that hung in the air was an intense alkaline and alcoholic mix that made the sheriff's eyes threaten to water. Both men were laid on tables beside one another, covered in linens that looked strange to Annabel. They were too clean. In her mind she could only picture the men in the state in which she had last observed them, hunks of bleeding and ragged meat on the floor of a cell. A cabinet and shelf near the back of the room held the personal effects of the two men, their clothes were neatly folded upon the shelf and their boots were neatly standing on the floor beneath them. Dim lamplight filled the room, and it felt claustrophobic and dark.

She stepped towards the tables and before her second step the doctor's gentle hand stopped her.

"Best you wash up first, please," he said, gesturing to a jar of clear liquid to her right. He placed both hands in the jar and shook them in the air before drying them on a cloth that hung on a hook beside the jar.

Annabel cleaned her hands and the liquid felt strangely cold once they were exposed to the air again. They reeked of alcohol so strong it made her cough. The marshal cleaned his hands as well and began to speak in a tone that sounded off to Annabel. The jovial and somewhat off-putting candor in his voice was absent and had been replaced with a clinical and measured tone.

"Now then, I promised you a lesson on speaking with the dead in a sense. This may be of interest to you as well, doctor."

Without another word he briskly stepped beside one of the sheets and withdrew it with a single tug. Beneath it rested a body Annabel did not recognize. Mr. Jeffries gasped and turned away at the sight.

The corpse's skin was an unnaturally pale grey color of old ashes. The whites of its eyes had gone a deep orange-yellow hidden behind half-lidded eyelids of bruised greyish-black. Lips pulled back from the teeth displayed yellowed teeth that looked like chips of discolored limestone set into deep violet-black gums. A thin black film flecked with what looked like bits of glittering metal coated the inside of the things' mouth, slick and glistening on its purple tongue.

Jeffries was shuddering and gasping in fear. Annabel could only stare, her lower lip trembling as her eyes raced from one grotesque feature to the next. She looked to the marshal, hoping for him to begin speaking comfort in his peculiar way, to explain what she was seeing. Yet he stood silently observing the body, a grim sentinel in a gray suit.

"*Good lord,*" the doctor muttered, backpedaling away from the corpse in fear. The physician stared dumbfounded at the bodies, both grey corpses were more vile than anything he had witnessed in years of medicine.

Turning to face the two still-living people in the room, the marshal wore an expression of purpose and determination so fierce it looked like he was wearing someone else's face.

"This thing on the table is no longer human. Both men had something else *inside* them. Something old, and very evil."

The doctor was leaning against the wall, as far away from the corpses as he could get. He stuttered with shuddering breath and tried several times to speak before abandoning the attempt altogether.

"This is what is loose out there, Sheriff. Believe me I wish it were not so, but there it is," the marshal said as he pointed at the ruined body on the table, "I can't stomach the thought that this may be that young girl's fate if we do nothing. We cannot allow it to continue poisoning the frontier any longer. We can stop it. Together."

Annabel looked at the macabre visage once more before turning to face away from it.

"Do you believe what I said before?" the marshal asked.

"Yes," the sheriff replied. She could hardly stand it, but he was right. Every ounce of sense she had told her it could not be true. That there were no such things as monsters. Yet upon that table lay a gray and rotting contradiction to those beliefs.

"I need to know where they met that stranger, and what their movements were over the last few days to find where they came into contact with the thing. If the girl is mixed up in this that makes *three locals* that have been infected. Whatever is happening here is only going to get worse. To do this I need to examine their effects."

The doctor didn't speak. He remained in the room and quietly observed. The marshal got to work and decided to give the doctor time to make his decision. He walked to the opposite side of the table to retrieve the shroud that had covered the strange deformed corpse and covered it up again.

"With luck we won't have to lift that again," he said, "I'd rather we take their belongings into the other room and work there where the light is better."

"I-I'll get their things, Marshal," the doctor spoke as if in a dream, walking trancelike towards the marshal to help him carry their clothes and boots.

"Is it catching?" Annabel asked, "Can we catch it from them by being so close?"

"It can't spread from person-to-person," the marshal answered, "My offices don't know much, but the case files make no mention of it. If it were catching, the valley would have been burned to the ground decades ago."

Annabel felt fingers of fear dancing down her back. She began to wonder what kind of things the Marshals were willing to do in their work against things like this.

"It comes from a source of some kind, likely close to Ganndo Valley or the surrounding prairie," he continued, "The substance that infects these people is either injected like venom from a snake or eaten like a poisonous mushroom. In both cases you'd have to be exposed to the source of the poison, the creature itself. Thankfully, whatever remains of it within its hosts dies when the host dies."

All three of the investigators left the terrors of the back room and retreated to the comfort of the main office lit by the sun. The doctor locked the door behind them, knowing the urge to do so was illogical, yet it comforted him all the same.

The marshal laid out the men's clothing and boots clinically on a table and produced a magnifying glass from one pocket, and his notebook and pencil from another.

The sheriff watched as the marshal checked the clothing's pockets and catalogued what was inside. He found a watch engraved with the initials *A.D*, for Amos Dweyer, he thought. A few spare matches. An empty tobacco poke. Each item written down with a few notes scribbled underneath it.

Sheriff Annabel checked their boots. Hidden in one was a cruel-looking curved knife, that looked more like a gutting knife for sheep than anything else. Regrettably, it bore no distinguishing marks. The soles of their boots were filthy and caked with thick dirt and pine needles.

She had long suspected that the two troublemakers had been living in the pines, but she could hardly pinpoint where among the countless acres of trees they had been hiding out.

"Crumble that dirt onto the table, would you?" the marshal asked, "And don't worry Mr. Jeffries, we'll clean up everything when we leave. And I mean *everything*."

The sheriff took the bootheel and thumped it on the table, crumbling the dirt and shaking it loose. Dried pine needles, grit, pebbles, and dirt cascaded onto the smooth wooden surface, piling up fairly substantially.

The marshal spread the dirt out with the side of a finger and examined it underneath the magnifying glass. He set the table aside and groaned in frustration.

54

"Not much to go on here, Sheriff. Rock, grit, and needles are so common out here I'd wager I'd find the same materials on every boot worn in this town."

"I'm not so sure..." Annabel said, gently taking the magnifier from him. She leaned close to the table to view the mess.

Underneath the lens she could see the tiny rock far more clearly. Little dark grey bits were inter-mixed with the rest of the gravel and limestone. A few of the specs glittered subtly, impossible to see by the naked eye.

"Well?" the marshal asked, "Anything jumping out at you?"

"Yeah," she replied, "There are far too many needles here to have been picked up in town, and there's this," she picked up a piece of the dark grey rock on a fingernail, moving aside for the marshal to view it under the glass.

"This is lead," she said, "More specifically, it's called galena. When they first tried to set up the silver mines out in the pines, they found almost no ore after the first few weeks of digging. Most of the silver had been gathered up in the first few days. Only one mine actually bore any real silver in quantities that could sell. Even then, most of it was intermixed with other junk ores, especially this. Usually in silver mining galena ore plays partner with large deposits of silver, but not in Ganndo Valley. Speculators left everything and went back east. Equipment and all."

"Meaning?" the marshal went on.

"Meaning these men were spending time in the old Emmet Mine. A whole lot of time, judging by how close to the heel the galena is packed. This buildup is from days walking over it," Annabel explained. The marshal smiled and nodded, impressed.

"Emmet Mine is dangerous, Sheriff," Mr. Jeffries said, stepping closer to the woman, "Most of the platforms are rotten through and the place is lousy with rattlers. Those three speculators that went back into it some years' ago to survey it again were never seen after they rode out that way. It's nothing more than a big evil pit in the earth. You can't go crawling around in there based on a hunch."

"It's all we've got, doctor," she retorted hotly, "They could have the girl down there. We have to try."

The bell at the door rang, interrupting the heated exchange. The undertaker stood in the open doorway, smoking a richly carved pipe.

"Everything alright, Leopold? I heard shouting," he said in a caramel smooth voice. Annabel saw the marshal's black eyes narrow. He clearly did not care for the undertaker, which was strange. Even in the saloon and in the aftermath of the shooting, he had been amicable with the criminals when he spoke. The behavior was off, and it made the sheriff wonder what it was the marshal sensed in the undertaker that made him bluster so.

"It's fine," Mr. Jeffries said, "Just working through some agitation from the action last night. The circumstances have made their way of raising tempers, but we're alright."

"Indeed, then," the undertaker said, "You have two more souls for me then later tonight? Once the police are done with them of course."

"Unfortunately, not, sir," the marshal said politely, "I plan on disposing of the bodies myself."

The undertaker looked stunned for a moment before regaining his senses.

56

"I'm sure if he were living, O'Toole would rather eat his hat than be put to rest by a government lawman."

"It's a good thing he's not living then, isn't it?" the marshal said, his words delivered in a somewhat sinister tone. The undertaker backed off with his palms raised and stepped back onto the porch through the open door.

"I get your meaning, marshal. Although if you plan on doing any more killing in this town, perhaps you'll let me know so I may make ready a few coffins," he nodded politely to the sheriff and the doctor after working his venomous words and departing.

"Good day Leopold. Sheriff."

After he left, the sheriff turned to the marshal to find him scribbling in his notebook. Once he finished hurriedly writing he looked up at Annabel.

"So then, our unpleasant exchange with that unsavory fellow notwithstanding, I believe we have our next lead. Emmet mine, then?"

The sheriff looked to Mr. Jeffries. The old physician sighed and gave her a tired and resigned smile.

"I know it's what you have to do. Just be careful, lass."

She approached the man and hugged him, which the marshal watched awkwardly before pretending to be busy studying the galena fragments again. Annabel didn't care if he saw her in this moment of vulnerability. She needed to let Mr. Jeffries know she would be alright.

"We will be," she said before releasing the man from the embrace. He smiled and adjusted his spectacles, looking at her with glittering and knowing eyes. She was tough. He knew that, just as he had known her to have proven her mettle time and time again in service to the old town. He felt a sense of relief knowing that the marshal would be with her.

"Marshal, we'll need to make our horses ready to ride out to the pines. The Emmet Mine is a good ride from town. We'll be spending a night on the trail at some point on our trip. Make any other arrangements you need today, and we'll set out immediately."

"Agreed. The only business I have left is to burn the blighted remains of these fellows and then I'll be along shortly," he added, intending to burn all traces of the monsters in the back room.

Annabel left the office behind to make for the stables and gather what they needed for their expedition into the great abandoned mine..

Chapter VI

Sheriff Annabel proceeded to the stables. She knew the ride out to the pines was over mostly flat land until the pastures ended and the grasses became thin and mired with rock. It promised to be an easy ride in weather like this. The prospect of what they might find buried in the old crumbling mine was not as easy to come to terms with.

Her skin felt alive in a gruesome way after what she saw in the doctor's office. The marshal had opened up the world to her in manner that shocked her to her core. His revelation peeled back the polished floorboards of her reality to reveal a writhing and scuttling infestation of insects beneath it. Now that she knew it was there, she could never look upon the world the same way. It made her wonder what else might be out there, lurking in unclaimed territory, waiting to be discovered as their nation's destiny was made manifest with its expansion to the far-off ocean.

She could count on fingers and toes how many times she had been needed out near the pines. There was really nothing out there worth a tinker's cuss to civilized folk unless they wanted to go about business unseen, hidden among the imposing spires of wood.

If her hunch about the galena was right, she and the marshal would have to venture *into* Emmet Mine. Despite what she told Mr. Jeffries, she knew it was dangerous. Yet she could not ignore the possibility that young Rosanna was down there.

Annabel reached the stables on the heels of that last thought and was bolstered with purpose and determination.

She untethered her own horse, a tawny-brown sixteen hands high Saddlebred named *Blunderbuss* that had served her well during her tenure as sheriff. The old stallion was getting on in years but had endurance that would rival a creature twice his weight and half his age, and Annabel had grown close to the animal over the years.

She set her saddle and tack and made sure her trusty .45 centennial rifle was secured upon it. The rifle had been a gift to her late father, and it served him well on his wagon journey out to settle in this pristine and quiet valley many years ago.

Reluctantly, she set her eyes at the back of the livery stable, to the stall where the marshal's horse was kept.

The beast had been stabled far away from the other horses, leaving a full empty stall between him and everything else in the barn. Even the cats wouldn't go near him.

He was a tiny thing, easily under fifteen hands, and a beautiful russet-black color. He carried his tail low and had high, proud withers, and his clean face bore glittering black eyes. He was a gorgeous horse, so much so that a few folks stopped and stared at the marshal when he rode into town upon the magnificent beast.

Annabel had no idea what breed he actually was. Her guess was that he was a barb of some kind or another, with a tiny drop of the devil in him.

The creature was *mean*. Worse yet, he was mean in a cunning way, as if it knew it was cruel and took delight in betraying the trust of other people and animals.

It seemed to get along with the marshal fine, but Annabel could tell it did not care much for people.

The sheriff didn't dream of trying to saddle the thing for the marshal, for fear of losing a finger. Or a hand. She'd wait until he had finished his business at the doctors for him to take care of it himself. She did want to inspect his tack, however. It was unlikely he was outfitted for a trip that far since they would have to camp outside overnight for the journey back. The marshal rode from the train station at which wasn't far, and the man may not be provisioned for a longer ride out. Where they were about to ride was rougher country, and Annabel wanted to be prepared. Lifting his saddlebags from a stall door, she examined his supplies.

Her examination was brief but enlightening. She always felt she could tell the cut of a man by what he took with him on travel. You could tell what a person found important, and tellingly, what he found non-essential. The marshal's tack was the uniform polished black leather that reeked of government issued equipment, that bore no markings for any division or company. Other than the plan saddle and some empty holsters, he had no trail gear to speak of at all. No bedroll, blankets, rations of any kind, nothing. How a man could travel overland, even for a day, without a tin and coffee was a mystery to Annabel. She considered a trip without it criminal. His saddlebags were laden only with a few scraps of paper and a box of matches that had been bent in half, with two loose sticks rolling around inside. She spied what might have been the remains of a twist of jerky, but the thing was so thin and odorless it could also be a bit of leather or string. A half-full canteen was the only item of any real use that was lashed to the saddle.

61

Both pistol holsters on the saddle were empty, yet there was a rifle of some sort housed in the rifle holster.

It was a piece of junk. Ill maintained and haggard, the old thing looked halfway to perdition in the state it was in. The lever on it looked almost rusted shut, and the barrel was scratched and scorched steel so far beyond blued she'd call it blackened. It looked like an old skillet. It lay in its holster like an insult to the pristine tack and glorious horse it would be seen with.

Oddly enough, Annabel did not recall seeing it with the marshal when he rode into town. She felt sorry for him thinking he may have purchased it in town.

"Am I set for the trail, partner?" she heard from behind her. The marshal was leaning in the wide barn doorway with his thumbs in his pockets, smiling slightly. In the orange light of midday, he looked surprisingly handsome, and Annabel felt her cheeks flush as she noticed him standing there. She cleared her throat awkwardly and moved her attention to the marshal's weapon in his saddle.

"This rifle will kill you," she said, "If it fires at all I'd suspect it would blow up in your face. I have a spare coach gun at the office, and I'm sure we could get you a fine centennial or Vetterli model from Duncan if I ask him nicely."

"No need ma'am," the marshal said calmly, moseying over to her, "I'm quite attached to that particular arm, and I mean to ride with it. My open-top is more than enough for any trouble we may encounter," he added with a pat on his hip and the pistol that rested there. He smiled at her and she felt another flutter in her stomach. The look on his face wasn't alien to Annabel, but was uncommon for her to see. She could tell by the way he looked at her that he was *really* looking at her. It was both flattering and inappropriate at the same time. It wasn't as if they were riding out to the prairie for an afternoon picnic. Concentrating on the task at hand, she quickly pulled the strap of the saddlebag shut and latched the clasp on the thing in haste.

"Suit yourself. We'll grab some more coffee and a spare blanket for you and head out."

Minutes later the two were saddled and mounted, riding at a brisk trot to the border of the town.

Turning into a field of grey and violet cotton overhead, the clouds twisted into strange tumultuous shapes that threatened rain. The two riders galloped onwards across the fields where lazy cattle grazed, the tall blades of wild grass cascading like an emerald ocean on either side of them as they went on their way.

A few farmers waved at the riders, and shouted salutations as they bolted past. After a brisk gallop, the horses slowed to a steady pace. Riding on through the day, they spoke little. Annabel observed the marshal while also minding the trail. Every hour or so, almost like a clockwork routine, the marshal withdrew his canteen and took quick sip and stowed it away. Annabel wondered if it was part of his marshal's training to do so. A desire to ask him about his work began growing in her mind, but she suppressed her curiosity. She wasn't sure she even wanted to know.

The silence out on the plain began taking its toll on Annabel's mind as the sun retreated from the heavens, working its magic that brought folks to talk when wandering its quiet expanses. By the time they settled down to camp, the marshal found his voice again.

"You want me to rope for snakes?" he asked, loosening a lasso from his saddle that Annabel was certain he didn't have with him before.

"No need," she replied, "Snakes out here are of a mild temperament. The fire should be enough to keep them away."

"I may still do it anyway," he said with that same obnoxious huckster grin he wore when talking sideways, pulling a thick paper package from his coat pocket, "It's not a bad habit to be prepared. A person doesn't get to be a marshal without having a good sense of preparation and routine."

"You been with the marshals long?" she asked, looking at him lazily adjusting his mustache and slicking back his raven hair. He fidgeted with the paper, unfolding it to reveal a thick stack of cold flapjacks, withdrawing one before passing them to Annabel. She took it and nodded with thanks. For trail rations, one could do a lot worse than Mrs. Mattingly's pancakes.

"Oh yes, indeed," he replied as he chewed, "Going on, let's see here, almost three years this October."

"Three years is a long time, huh?" she said wryly while she set up the coffee tin. He grinned.

"For my division it is quite a long tenure. In fact, I should count myself lucky for it. The kind of work I am given often carries a certain amount of risk."

"Risk like this?" she said abruptly, before being able to stop herself and phrase the question more artfully. The marshal's eyes went wide, and he blinked hard. After a moment he shook his head, making a sputtering sound.

"*Absolutely not*," he exclaimed, "Mostly I deal with other humans, men or women playing with forces that they oughtn't. I had thought I'd been witness to some strange and miraculous things, but this is a completely alien adversary. What troubles me most is that the old case files, the details of the first encounter with the thing, were *incredibly* out of sorts. Bits and pieces of it were just plain missing, entire swaths of accounts and details were plucked out of it, almost on purpose. I shudder to think that perhaps someone possessed might have made it into our offices back east. It makes a man feel like he's changed somehow just knowing it exists, something that can creep up beside you wearing another man's skin."

Annabel stared down at the green and grey earth as a way to ground herself and her thoughts. She knew exactly what the marshal meant. It was hard to imagine ever feeling happy again, knowing evils like this are alive in the world. The woman became quiet, lamenting the innocence and ignorance she lost mere hours ago.

Black and glinting, secretive and world-weary, the marshal's eyes looked to her. The lawman felt partly responsible for bringing her into the strange world in which he lived and fought. A lovely young woman, whose life was already dominated by service to the law, now beaten down with more responsibility as a party that knows strange evils lurk in the dark.

"Hey now Sheriff, it is not the doom of hope to know these things. If anything, it's life-affirming in a way. It makes simple comforts more valuable, and makes you cherish the pleasant things that much more. Coffee and flapjacks by a campfire, for example. Every good thing, every happy memory and experience, all stand united and opposed to the darkness that lies hidden out on the frontier. It makes you want to make the most of every pure moment as you can, to give *everything* you can to bring more love into the world. I live loudly, some might say foolishly. But I do it to spite these strange and evil things. I do it to prove that evil will *never win*, and that the human spirit is indomitable, human love is indivisible."

The sheriff couldn't help but smile, looking at the marshal's ridiculous expression as he said it with his cheeks full of pancakes, grinning like a loon.

"That sounds practiced."

"Pretty good, isn't it?" he grinned wildly. Annabel spit and poured their coffee.

"You aren't really a marshal, are you?" she asked, taking another drink, "Marshals are lawmen in places even more remote than Ganndo Valley. They aren't whatever it is you are."

"Oh, I'm a marshal all right," he said grinning, "Not the same bureau as the one set up by the federal government back after the revolution, but similar enough."

"I doubt that," Annabel quipped. She set her cup beside her and looked over the marshal again. He looked like any generic federal officer, but it was almost *too* generic, like it was done on purpose as a kind of joke.

"Honest truth," the man swore with his hand on his vest, "We're more or less a global organization. We've been known by other names in other places over the years, but here in New World, we're called marshals. We hunt down wanted undesirables, serve writs and warrants to illicit occult parties, investigate happenings that are unnatural or unexplained. Things like that. It's not so different from other kinds of law. Just different. Older."

"How did you find yourself doing this kind of work?" Annabel asked while she rolled a cigarette. For a moment, the marshal became quiet as well, gazing at the fire and then up at the clear night sky. He sniffed the cool air and shook himself out of his melancholy and looked Annabel in the eye again.

"It's complicated, as many things like this are. Almost every marshal joins up because they saw something. Once that world opens up to you, it's hard to close the doors on it."

"Does anyone ever do that?" Annabel said nervously, thinking of herself and how her life would never be the same, "Close the doors on it, I mean."

The marshal refilled his cup with water from his canteen and took a long drink before answering. Annabel lit her cigarette and took a slow pull from it, studying the man before he answered.

"A few," he finally admitted, "Folks who get out usually get out early. It's like that cigarette you've got there. Easier never to start than it is to quit, and the longer you go on doing it, the harder it gets."

"What about me? What happens to me, to the valley, if we kill this thing?"

"Things return to normal, I'd suspect," the marshal said, "Although without this creature swallowing up travelers and drifters, you'll see more folks coming around from the rail. Once they taste that whiskey some of them might even stay. You might get more outlaws out this way too. Might be a good idea to start looking at bringing on a deputy or two."

"I don't work well with others," Annabel said with a sharp grin. The marshal laughed.

"Present company excluded I hope," he said wryly.

"We'll see."

Crickets continued singing in their strange ringing tones that lingered in the night air. Annabel set down her cup and sighed heavily, breathing out a plume of white smoke that twisted and turned as it disappeared in the air.

"Do you ever think about it?" she asked the marshal.

"Think about what?" he said, turning to face her again with the stars reflected in his obsidian eyes.

"Giving it up. Living a normal life. If I need a deputy after this is over, I could think of worse choices than you."

"I'm not so sure," he said, twisting his moustache, "That young Henry Colm has some grit."

"I mean it," she said awkwardly, not sure how to phrase what she was trying to say, and even less certain she should be saying it at all, "You obviously like it here, and it has to be better than this terror and horror you see with the Marshals. Why keep doing it?"

Pausing for a moment, the man opened his mouth to answer and was at a loss for words. He chuckled and then looked confused and concerned all at one, rubbing the bridge of his nose with his thumb and forefinger, searching for a response.

"Partly," he said, starting over after another pause, "Partly because I like it. I really do. I get to see and do things that really make a difference. It's like, it's like knowing the truth about the world. It feels more real, somehow. It makes everything more real, and that much more worth holding onto."

He kicked gently at the rocks at the edge of the fire, feeling foolish for not being able to explain it better to the sheriff.

"I swore an oath when I joined the Marshals, and I believe in that just as much now as I did back then. What we're doing is true. It's noble. It's who I am. Before I am anything else, I'm a marshal."

"Neither rain nor sleet, huh?" Annabel said, somewhat disappointed he didn't consider her offer, if it even was an offer at all.

"Something like that," he laughed, rubbing the back of his neck, "Would you like to hear it?"

Sheriff Annabel nodded. The marshal sat up straight and adjusted his mustache as he closed his eyes briefly. When they re-opened, they were alive with purpose.

"We are the nameless,

The riders in the night.

We are the faceless,

Who raise the shining light.

We are the fearless,

And never shall we fall,

We are the marshals,

That keep watch over all."

Once he finished, he looked somewhat bashful about it, and quickly added,

"Of course, it sounds better with the pomp and circumstance of a more official accompaniment from the office itself. But you get the idea."

"No, I like it," Annabel said seriously, "It really is noble, Marshal. I hope you find peace with it once we're through with this monster. Maybe I'll find some peace after this all ends, too."

Unable to find something believable enough to reassure her, the marshal smiled and nodded quietly.

The night passed them by slowly, and after a time they both were fast asleep beside the fire, blanketed by the stars.

Chapter VII

The next morning after coffee and another few pancakes, the pair saddled up to continue their ride out to the woods. This time neither one of them spoke on the trail as they drew closer to the forest.

With a nod, the sheriff drew the marshal's attention to the woods ahead. Towering high and ancient, the trees stood unbent against the slowly mounting wind.

She brought her horse to a stop at the edge of where the land sloped downwards slightly towards the forest. The black demon the marshal rode stopped as well, glaring hatefully at the firs. Annabel checked her rifle and cocked the lever action to chamber a round. Her eyes fell on the weathered rifle in the marshal's saddle.

"The mine is back through the woods. We'll be riding through some thick cover. If Dweyer and O'Toole were outlawed up out here, there could be trouble. That mangled long gun of yours actually shoot?"

"From horseback I wouldn't chance firing a rifle," the marshal replied. He drew his revolver and took the reins in his left hand.

Sheriff Annabel shook her head and led *Blunderbuss* further into the thick of the trees with the marshal close behind. High above them crows called out to one another and the wind howled as it picked up steam.

The sheriff was tense. She gripped her rifle tightly and eyed the treacherous and crowded terrain. There were hundreds of places to hide in these woods. Crags and small caves pitted the undergrowth, gaping stone mouths that swallowed darkness whole, each of them large enough to conceal multiple persons. She imagined bandits inside every hollow, lurking beyond every portal of rock, waiting like vipers to strike from places unseen.

The marshal's horse hissed, it actually *hissed* like a serpent at the very moment Annabel finished her thought comparing hiding men to vipers. It turned sharply away from where the marshal was leading it and bared glittering white teeth, refusing to move.

"Ah cheese and crackers," he said with a defeated tone before leading the horse to a nearby tree and dismounting.

"What are you doing?" Annabel asked, subconsciously cradling the rifle in both hands now. She stopped herself just shy of leveling her weapon at the marshal's horse. It just wasn't natural behavior for a stallion to act the way it did. It frightened her.

"He won't go any further," the marshal grunted, tying the reigns around the tree. "Too many gopher holes and snake pits ahead. He's liable to break a leg in a pitted mire like that."

"How do *you* know that? I thought you've never been out the Ganndo Valley before."

"I haven't. But he knows it. The noise he made means snakes and snake pits. I've ridden with him long enough to know."

72

Skeptical and still extremely uncomfortable with the creature's actions, Annabel shrugged. She honestly felt safer with him tied up. Dismounting herself, she tied her own horse to another tree, far from the black horse. Over her shoulder she could see the marshal pull his own damaged rifle from the saddle very carefully, and he set it over his shoulder, securing it with a black leather strap. Annabel shook her head and snorted.

"Awfully impolite to go on laughing at me like that, ma'am. I pray we won't need it at all, but a man doesn't get this far in my line of work without being careful. Lead the way."

They continued on foot.

The marshal, or his horse, Annabel supposed, was correct. The path ahead was rife with small holes and pits, some of which were so deep she could not see the bottom of them. What was stranger was the parts of the ground that were even to walk upon. They felt strange. Almost wrong in a way. The sheriff couldn't quite explain it, but the sensation was strange. It felt like the ground was too dry. Like it was giving underfoot. It reminded her of walking over frozen streams as a child, and of her father warning her to wait until it had frozen all the way to the bottom.

"When they started blasting out here for the mine, I suppose they knocked a fair amount of earth loose. The ground beneath us feels weak, Marshal. Treacherously so."

Before he could quip or ramble on about it, the marshal cried out as the earth beneath him crumbled and gave way.

"Sheriff!" he shouted, his voice buried underneath the tumultuous sound of crumbling earth and rock. In a moment, the marshal had disappeared, slipping into the pit that had opened beneath him. A loud series of noises like crackling tinder followed the sounds of destruction. From far below her, Annabel heard the marshal growling in pain. Where he stood a moment ago there was a great hole in the earth. Roots and grass protruded from crumbling dirt that formed a ring of solid ground around the gaping pit ahead.

"Are you alive down there?!" Annabel shouted, peering down at the man from where she was standing. She didn't move. Her bootheels were rooted to the spot. She didn't want to chance the unstable ground.

At the bottom of the newly opened ravine, the marshal rolled over onto his back and sucked air through his teeth sharply.

"I am alive but unwell!" he growled, his forehead already beading with sweat from the pain, "Something is broken. My arm. I can't see it, and I daren't move again."

Searching for a safe path down to the man, the sheriff turned towards the direction they came. A thick and ancient pine stood perhaps fifteen paces away. Its roots had to be deep and strong, strong enough to be on stable footing. If she could reach it and tie a rope around it, she could climb down to where the marshal lay.

But to reach it, she would have to walk back over to it. Annabel swallowed hard. She had no idea where she stepped to reach this spot. A wrong move could cause another collapse, which could bury the marshal alive in addition to injuring her.

Fifteen paces, and no room for error.

Taking a deep breath, the sheriff carefully stepped forward towards the pine.

She put her weight down gradually as her boot came to rest. The ground held. Concentrating, she lifted her back foot and brought it forward to continue moving. From out of sight, she heard the marshal groan again. His breathing was loud enough for her to hear now. She had to move quickly. Bracing herself, she took another step.

Her concentration was broken by the sound of gunfire.

A thunderous crack from below was followed shortly after by the sound of a second shot. Ringing out over the hills and trees, the sounds bounced around before settling as it faded into silence.

"Marshal!" she cried out, turning and looking over the edge of the maw before her. She couldn't see below anymore, and he did not reply after the gunshot. He could be dead.

Turning back to face the tree, her pace quickened. Careful but with haste, she continued until she reached the trees. She stepped to her horse and withdrew a thick cabled rope. Her hands were still and strong despite her fear, she had trained them well. She lashed the rope to the trunk and walked carefully back to the edge where the marshal fell.

Trembling hatefully beneath her, the ground groaned and crackled, but held.

Annabel peered down into the chasm.

The marshal lay unmoving in the pit. His rifle was in his right hand, and the barrel was still trailing steel-blue smoke in thin wisps. There was no telling what he shot at.

"Marshal speak to me!" she called. No reply

Swearing, the young woman took the rope in her hands and edged herself closer to the crumbling precipice. She pulled hard on the rope and checked that it was secure before throwing it down into the newly formed cavern. Like a chameleon testing a limb, she eased one foot off of solid ground, and lowered herself on her stomach, taking the rope between her strong thin hands. She began to climb down, sliding a little at a time until she reached the bottom. Her boots hit the ground and splashed in something wet. She peered down and was relieved to find it wasn't blood, but rather water that had collected below ground.

Hurrying to the marshal, she knelt beside him and sucked her teeth when she saw him up close.

His suit jacket and left sleeve were stained with blood. Blooms of red had spread to his undershirt as well, and his face was slate gray. The fingers of his left hand were pale brown and unmoving.

She brushed her hair behind one ear and leaned in close to his face. The man was breathing, but the sound of it was weak and fluttering.

There was no way she could climb out with him. She could tie the rope to his body and use her horse to pull him up, but she didn't dare chance doing so. If anything were broken inside him, a rib or his spine, pressure from the line could make it worse.

Looking beside the marshal, there was a thick track of earth that had been scorched with intense heat that trailed off into the darkness of the cave they had fallen into. It looked like it stopped just shy of reaching the man, and Annabel wondered what the hell happened. The rock was still hot beside the wounded man.

From the blackness, she could smell something savory but somewhat sickening. It smelled like charred meat.

Standing up, she walked deeper into the cave and gasped in alarm when she saw it.

It was another man, and he'd been burned alive.

Blackened flesh so blistered it looked like charcoal clung loosely to charred bones, which were yellowed and scorched with heat. Melted eye sockets stared up at the cavern ceiling, set above a nose-less face grimacing with shockingly clean white teeth. The corpse's right wrist ended in a thin ragged stump near the remains of a revolver that looked as if it had exploded in his hand. A few errant trails of smoke were still rising from the body, being blown back into the shadows.

She looked at the marshal's battered old gun and at once knew what had happened and felt sickened at the thought of the marshal using such a sinister weapon, while also wondering how such a thing could be done. It looked like a horrible way to die.

"Oh Penelope, I am finished," the marshal croaked from behind Annabel. She turned and quickly stumbled to kneel at his side.

"No Marshal, it's me, Annabel. The sheriff, remember? I need to know if you can walk."

His eyes slowly opened into small slits, his black irises glittering beneath his lashes.

"I'm hurt bad, miss," he said in a whisper, reaching with his intact hand. Annabel took it in her own hands, hoping to comfort the man.

"Back in Pixie, they said I'd not get the death I wanted. Damned card-readers," he smiled, weakly and pitifully, his lip trembling, "I reckon this isn't so bad. Seeing as you're with me, love."

"You're not going to die, you ridiculous fop," the sheriff grumbled as she lightly squeezed his hand, "Stay awake and help me figure how to get you back to the valley."

"Fine whiskey in the valley," he mumbled, "Heard tale all the way in Tecumac...finest a man can enjoy."

With one last shake, he lay still and quiet. Still breathing, but just barely.

"Damn it," Annabel growled, kicking at the dirt. There was a new sound behind her, near the burned man's body. She heard the click of a gun's hammer, and the sound of several men making sounds of revulsion intermixed with snickering and laughter.

"Your friend is busted up pretty bad ma'am."

Slowly, she reached for her revolver at her hip before the voice behind her spoke again.

"You leave that iron there, or there'll be three bodies left for the coyotes."

She turned to look and saw six armed men standing in the mouth of the cave, all with weapons at the ready. One thin man stood in front of the rest and grinned with malice while pointing his revolver at her.

"Now let's see what we can do about you and your friend."

Chapter VIII

Men in torn clothes that reeked of soot and grime led her down farther into the caverns where the rock was a ragged and dangerous landscape with razor sharp edges.

Her gun was taken almost immediately, and her nose was bleeding from where they struck her. She had tried to stop them from moving the marshal, and in the tussle one of them smashed her in the face with the butt of his pistol. It took three of them to stop her though, and the sheriff took some small pride in that. She was almost certain she was going to die down here in the mines. It was a comfort to feel good about something.

Twisting drunkenly downward, the trail made a tangled path the bandits followed as they brought Annabel deeper into the earth. Soon the cavern narrowed, and she began to see a few lights from weak lanterns ahead. She suspected he cave must meet up with Emmet Mine.

She had never been *inside* the mines before but knew immediately after she had entered them that Mr. Jeffries concerns with the place were well-founded.

Rotted support beams and splintering wooden pillars protruded at awkward angles, barely supporting the tons and tons of rock overhead. Lanterns were held aloft from these beams, hanging from rough hooks made from twisted nails that had been worked to form a crude loop of iron. In one section of the walkway she saw what she believed to be a pool of blood on the floor.

"Go on then, stop gawking!" one of the outlaws snarled, pushing her forward with the barrel of her own stolen revolver. Ste stepped forward, keeping quiet. They had left her hands unbound, which in quarters this tight wouldn't matter. But if the path opened up a bit, and she could steal a moment, the sheriff could make a play to grab the gun and shoot the bastards before they could do anything about it.

The had the marshal's strange rifle as well, but they neglected to take his pistol, which even now was holstered and concealed in his jacket. The men carrying him were too far ahead in the narrow passage for her to reach it though. Her best bet was her own gun. If she made a play for anything, that would be it.

A move like that right now, she'd be shot in an instant. Of course, there was also the marshal to consider. If he were still alive, she couldn't risk further harm coming to him.

Deeper down they delved, and the air was hot and thick, as if the earth itself was having difficulty breathing. A film of greasy sweat began to form on Annabel's forehead. Down this far no one would find her body, the sun would never shine on her grave in this horrible place.

"You boys plan actually know where you're going?" she growled, frustrated and hateful. Desperation moved her tongue, desperation for any kind of display of humanity from her otherwise silent captors.

"Shut up," the leader said, "There's steps to take in this thing. Not that one of *you* would understand," he grinned at her, his yellowed-gray teeth shining in the ugly lantern light of the passage, "It's a dance, missy. A song and dance, and you get to be a part of it. Be grateful we didn't just shoot you in the cave. Especially after you roasted poor Earl alive."

A croaking, thick, coughing filled the cave, followed by jeers and howls from the other bandits.

At last the passage opened to reveal a circular chamber, pitted with wide holes on all sides, and two other exits from the room. This cistern must have been where the majority of the blasting stopped back when the mine was first opened. Worn worm-eaten barrels of meal were left open and stinking near one passage, while another displayed a broken-down minecart laden with rusted tools.

From above, tangled roots grew in a webbed mass that spread across the cavern ceiling and hung low enough that the sheriff could touch them if she jumped. Three lanterns lit the room, and the shadows down here were as thick and dark as the humid stinking air.

Freshly used equipment, picks, shovels, and carts, were strewn about the room. It was clear these men had not only been outlawed up in this place but were working on mining down in the dark. Judging by the number of tools and the sheer amount of crumbled rock, they were digging much deeper than the mine had originally gone.

In the center of the room was a sort of altar carved from the stone itself, and Annabel's eyes went wide with terror when she saw the girl lying on it.

"What did you do to her!" she screamed, throwing her elbow into the man behind her like a sledgehammer. Pushing forward, she tried to squeeze past the other men to reach the girl. One of

81

the bandits grabbed a handful of her hair while another squeezed her throat and pressed the cold steel of a revolver to gut.

"Another outburst like that and you're a dead woman, you hear!"

"Not yet, you idiot," said another voice, "We can't kill her. People will talk if the sheriff goes missing. It's almost time, we only have to wait a little longer now."

Manic with fury, she craned to see over the attackers. Rosanna was still unmoving, either asleep or dead. The sheriff was pushed hard onto the ground in the chamber, and her knees and palms were cut by the wickedly sharp rock. The marshal's body was dumped on the ground beside her, thumping limply on the ground.

Hot tears streaked down Annabel's cheeks, still red with rage. These people were not men, they were beasts. No more than dogs that she desperately wanted to put down.

"Don't cry, sweet Annabel. All is well…"

Sound vanished from the mine. The bandits were silent, their heads bowed briefly as they stopped moving. Annabel looked up at the altar, where the voice had come from.

Rosanna sat upright, the movement of her body liquid and smooth. She turned and looked at Annabel with her tiny eyes glittering in the dim lantern's glow.

"Do not be afraid. Down here we are all safe."

Too stunned to speak, the sheriff stared at the girl. Her skin was ashen gray that intensified into a coal black color in places around her joints. Even in the dim conditions Annabel could see something was wrong with her.

"Rosanna, whatever these men have done to you we can fix it. Mr. Jeffries will take care of you, just like before, remember? You had that spill by the canyon gorge when you were little, and he patched you right up. You were so brave then," Annabel carefully got to her feet, watching both the girl and the bandits.

"My flesh was weak then," the young girl said wistfully, "But I am better now. I'm *more*. I found this place all by myself, it's been my own secret place ever since I was small. Even before I could hear the choir, deep down. The Elder called me here with voices in the earth, with a choir of hope. He just wanted us to be a part of him. A part of something more."

She slithered off of the alter and onto the floor in a heap, her joints turning awkwardly as she slipped to the ground. The girl moved unnaturally, as if she her bones were broken inside. She began to crawl towards Annabel.

"I had something to offer him, something *new*. I gave him new ideas... I showed him veins of wood and metal. I brought *them* here, too," she whispered, her long-fingered hands twitching as they dragged her desiccated gray mass across the sharp cavern floor, leaving a trail of blood and tarlike slime behind her. The bandits watched her as men enraptured, gazing upon the misshapen girl with holy reverence.

"My new friends who were camped out above the mine, simple men with simple aims. I lured them down here with me with whispers and promises. I brought them here...to *him*. Now we are at peace, united as many minds into one."

Annabel was no longer crying now. The girl she set out to save was gone. Only this thing remained, like a shadow in the shape of the girl. There would be time to mourn her later... if she survived this. Right now, all Annabel could feel was the building fires in her chest, beginning to crackle and roar with the sounds of bloody retribution.

"Many into one, huh? Like Dweyer and O'Toole?" Annabel spat through gritted teeth. She wanted to back away from the slowly approaching thing that once was Rosanna but would not leave the marshal's side.

"They were pitiful, wretched little things," the girl muttered, her voice shuddering and croaking, "They wanted to be silent and apart. Un-joined with us. They fled their glorious becoming. We sent someone to collect them and bring them back inside. With the one that is many... You don't need to be alone anymore, Annabel," her head twisted upwards crookedly, her cheeks thin and cadaverous. Her teeth where yellowed and malformed, set into purple and black slime-ridden gums.

"It has taken so long to spread across this country of men. But now he has a smarter way. A *better* way. You don't know it yet, but we need to be united like this. He's coming back. Humanity has to be ready. We cannot stand divided against what's coming."

Annabel faltered, taking a single step in retreat. She could not hope to confront this *thing* and a roomful of armed men. This was it. The end of the line. From beside her on the ground, the marshal coughed.

The creature stopped crawling, cocking her head sideways and making her spine crackle and crunch, staring at Annabel.

"Come inside with us."

"It sounds pretty crowded in there already, miss," the marshal said, grinning slightly with one eye open as he raised his head.

Rolling onto his side, the man flipped over and drew his pistol. He fanned the hammer and fired all six rounds, so fast it looked almost as if he fired them all at once. He sunk three bullets into the creeping thing that was approaching him, blowing apart her grey inhuman flesh into reeking chunks that sprayed across the altar in sickening violet red and black swatches. His next three shots put one into each of the lanterns which hit home with a crash, blasting the glass and iron apart and plunging the cavern into absolute darkness.

The bandits screamed and wailed, men now hysterical with what Annabel was shocked to recognize as grief. They sobbed and sniffled, dribbling black mucous and shuddering hideously in the dark.

"Mother! Oh mother! What have they done!"

"Kill them, rip them, eat their flesh! Swallow their teeth!" their mad voices and cries echoed off of the cavern walls, sounding somehow amplified in the absolute darkness.

"Death! Devour their souls!"

From the ground beside her, she heard the marshal struggling to reload, muttering weakly.

"That's our signal to get out of here, partner. Here," she felt him press his pistol gently against her boot, "Take it and go. Be careful feeling your way out...Rocks are sharp. You take good care of my horse for me."

Reaching down, Annabel too the revolver in one hand and the marshal's forearm in the other.

"Get up. We're both getting out of here."

The marshal tried and failed to stifle a scream as Annabel pulled him to his feet. Roaring from beneath the mine came a voice that shook the firmament itself with malevolent power.

"There! I hear them! Bring them to me!"

With a mind of its own, the sheriff's hand swung in the direction of the nearest screaming possessed outlaw and fired.

The muzzle flash was so bright it was blinding in the dark, and Annabel struggled to keep her head, pulling the stumbling and wounded marshal with her towards what she hoped was the exit. She turned around carefully, putting her heels together to turn in the opposite direction of the altar and the horrors around it.

A roar erupted from beside her, and at once one of the bandits was upon her, flailing with his hands and gnashing his teeth in the utter blackness, tearing at her shirt as he bit her. Annabel stabbed the pistol at his gnashing face and pulled the trigger. In a flash the man's head exploded, and she heard the marshal cough and chuckle.

"Hey, he had my rifle."

Annabel took it from the dead man and leveled the weapon, turning it around to face the direction she had been coming from, towards the altar. She stuffed the marshal's pistol into her own empty holster at her side and worked the lever of the heavy gun.

"Anna don't!" the marshal cried, but it was too late.

She fired the weapon, and a jet of flame erupted from the barrel with a thunderous roar, making the weapon so hot Annabel almost dropped it. The cavern came alive with fire. Two bandits screamed as they burst into flames, flailing wildly as they tumbled around. The hanging roots overhead caught as well, illuminating the cavern, and filling it with choking black smoke.

Not wasting a moment, the sheriff pulled the marshal with her, heading towards the nearest passage going as fast as she could while leading him along. From behind her she heard gunfire, rounds sliced through the air and ricocheted off of the cave walls, flashes like lightning could be seen in the thick clouds of smoke she left behind.

Stumbling and panting, Anna wiped the sweat from her brow as she kept on moving, heedless of the sounds of bedlam from behind her.

Ahead, she could see a lantern unlit near what looked like ramp leading out. The path became dark as she got farther and farther away from the raging fire in the cistern chamber. Reaching the end of the path, she stopped.

Dead end. She saw no sunlight, and in the dark could not find a doorway.

The marshal's panicked breathing had slowed again, and he was carrying less of his own weight, leaning heavily on Annabel.

"Did we make it?" he asked in the slightest of whispers, his tone of voice desperate yet hopeful.

Annabel did not reply. She leaned back against the jagged rock wall, defeated. Her head leaned back and thumped against something smooth with a neat corner on it.

Blindly reaching upwards, she felt the heavy bracing of a worn-out support block. Above it was a heavy door made of slatted wood, with a heavy metal latch on it.

She laughed in disbelief, feeling the rush of adrenaline making her giddy and lightheaded.

Straining her exhausted and shredded muscles she pulled at the latch, shaking the doorway free and flooding the chamber with dirt. She coughed and choked and felt as if they would be buried alive. But the cascading earth finally yielded, and beyond the edge of the doorway the barest sliver of sunlight crept in, orange and dying. Had they reached this juncture even a few minutes later, the night sky would have disguised this escape route and doomed them both.

She began to dig, making enough room to crawl halfway out. Her eyes squinted hard as they adjusted to the light, faint as it was. She reached down and hauled the marshal up, groaning with effort and she pulled the fully grown man up the slope of ragged dirt. After she got him out, she crawled free herself, and kicked at the dirt around the doorway until it was completely blocked and covered once more.

Overhead the pines blew carelessly in the breeze, uncaring and unaware of what had transpired deep beneath their roots. Sheriff Annabel's momentary adrenaline high quickly faded as she looked around. While it was true that they had both escaped with their lives, they were now lost. Surrounded on all sides by unfamiliar territory, with only a dying man as company, Annabel found little hope left in her weary and tired heart. Night fell upon them.

Chapter IX

Jolted awake by the haunting song of an owl, Annabel drew the marshal's pistol from her holster and painfully sat upright.

The woods were dark and cold. It was late, and overhead a cover of lazy black clouds completely cloaked the moon, revealing it only in slivers beneath its waves. Scant light to see by came from faint and winking stars drawn behind the cumulous veil of clouds from moment to moment.

Annabel shivered and drew her jacket closed with her free hand while she still held her pistol. The nights were cold here, and she could see her breath before her as a white mist in the air. She was thirsty and cold, and her body still ached from the battle in the mines. It was unlikely she and the marshal could be followed by the raving cult from below ground, but she took no chances with it.

The marshal had not moved from where she placed him after they emerged lying upon the ground, silent and still.

There was nothing Annabel could do for him. She didn't know anything about doctoring and surely couldn't hope to carry or drag the man back to Ganndo Valley. If she could even find it. If she left him alone in the woods, there was no guarantee she could find him again. She looked to the pistol in her hand.

Across the pitch of trees and rock there was another sound, and it was certainly not an owl.

The sheriff squinted and scanned the tree line. In the distance, silhouetted against the midnight sky was a horse. The creature's pelt was darker than even the night sky behind it, and the animal stood like a void in space, a black paper cutout against the landscape.

Snorting again, the thing approached, and as Annabel recognized what it was her fear subsided, although she remained afraid.

It was the marshal's horse. It drew closer, and the sheriff could see its black leather reigns dangling from beside its snout, as if it had bitten through them to break free of its ties.

How the thing found Annabel and its master she could not guess.

Hooves stepped heavily upon small bits of rock and wood, cracking them underfoot with powerful strides. In moments it loomed over the marshal, staring down at the motionless man.

Eyes black and cold stared at the marshal. Annabel watched without moving, hesitant to startle the beast or to distract it from whatever it was doing. It snorted and sent a plume of steam into the air. Time trickled by slowly. The beast looked as if it was considering whether to leave the man behind or not. Under the strain of the uncomfortable silence, Annabel spoke to the thing.

"You are a strange and otherworldly beast. I could tell that much back in the stables. So now you've gotten free, what are you going to do? Are you going to help us or not?"

90

It hissed like a snake again, possibly weighing its options. After some consideration it looked to the marshal and back to the sheriff before it turned its head oddly to the side. Like it wanted her to follow it.

Annabel hoped her feelings on the creature's intent were correct. She knelt down beside the marshal and struggled to lift the man. He made no sound as she did so. Awkwardly trying to hold him over her shoulder, she managed to lay his body over the horse's saddle. It allowed her to place the man upon its back, and as soon as she had finished it began to walk away. The sheriff followed.

In the dark she had a difficult time reckoning which direction they were heading and had no way of knowing if the path the horse was leading her on even went back to town at all. Placing her trust in the black stallion, she pressed on with their march through the darkened pines.

They walked for what felt like hours to the sheriff. She could see the moon moving overhead throughout their journey and before long, her calves began to burn with the effort of it. She still could not see any sign of dawn and wondered if they would be walking until the sun wormed its way into the sky.

The trees became sparser as they went along their way, until Annabel could at last see the plains opening up before her, illuminated by the orange and violet light of tomorrow.

The plains were open and featureless, save for a single lone cabin set amidst the empty land. They were nowhere near any part of the frontier that she had seen, and certainly not any closer to the valley. Feeling betrayed by her guide and foolish on the heels of the thought that a horse somehow deceived her, she stopped in place. The horse kept going.

"You've led us out here into unfamiliar territory to die, is that it?!" she shouted at the beast. Heedless of her cries, the horse sauntered onward towards the cabin in the far distance. She gritted her teeth and spat onto the ground, fuming with anger. A moment later, she saw a light coming from the cabin, in the shape of an opened door. Perhaps they heard her shouting.

"Help!" she called, her voice cracking with thirst that had been awakened with the prospect of a drink, "Help! My friend is injured! I'm calling for aid if you can hear me!"

Ahead of her the black horse whinnied in a deep and resonant tone, which sounded to Annabel like mocking laughter. Almost like the horse was making fun of her distrust of it.

"Fine, you great beast, you were right I suppose," she muttered, mustering up the strength to jog ahead to walk beside the horse once more. A lantern swung in the hand of a stranger ahead that had emerged from the cabin. After a few long minutes, she got close enough to see the figure in the newborn sunlight.

The man was gaunt and old, with tanned skin that looked worn and cracked in the sun like untreated leather. In one hand the man held a sawn-off scattergun, and in the other hand he held the lantern. Annabel tried not to react upon closer inspection. The man's right arm ended halfway down the forearm, and in its place was a domed metal cap with a hook set upon it that kept the lantern aloft. A series of belts and straps attached the apparatus to the stump of his arm.

He wore a wide brimmed straw hat and an oversized wool duster that dragged through the grass and timothy that grew in patches on the plain. Wisps of breath blew out from under the brim every few moments.

"I'll have your name before you get any closer, boy," the man said in a tinny voice, leveling the shotgun to face Annabel. Both barrels gleamed in the early morning light, the steel so finely polished they looked alive with orange fire.

"I'm Sheriff Annabel Hawke of Ganndo Valley, I'm a woman, not a boy. My friend and I are injured and disordered and in need of aid."

"I didn't know they had women sheriffs nowadays," the man said with skepticism. Annabel's brow furrowed, and she felt the temptation prickling in her fingertips, begging her to pull leather.

"I suppose things change in a hurry out east," the man said after a pause, lowering his weapon, "You come on and git inside. I'll start a tin of coffee and see to your pal on the horse."

He turned to walk back towards his cabin, clearly trusting that Annabel wouldn't shoot him in the back. She followed the man alongside the black horse until they reached the porch. She subconsciously went to reach for the horse's chewed up reigns to tie him to the porch before scoffing at her own foolishness and left it be.

The thin man opened the door with a creak and waved with the shotgun to usher the sheriff inside. The smell of the cabin wafted out invitingly, reeking of molasses and coffee beans. Annabel swallowed her hunger and buried her thirst and she walked past the man indoors. He set the lantern on a small desk near the door before stepping to the horse and pulling the marshal gently off of the thing's saddle, throwing him over one shoulder. Annabel stared, forgetting her manners as she watched a man that she would wager weighed no more than one hundred pounds carry the marshal like a sack of cornmeal into the cabin.

Stalking past the girl, the man set the marshal onto a bed in the corner of the room and sucked his teeth.

"You do this to him?" he asked casually, approaching the cabin's sloppily mortared stone chimney and kneeling to place a few logs into it.

"No. He slipped in the pines and fell on his arm. I think it's broken."

"You think, do you?" the thin man said with a short and mean spirited laugh as he struck a match and set the logs aflame, he blew out the match and stood, approaching a round wooden cabinet.

"His clothes reek of gunpowder. As do yours. You do a lot of shooting before or after he slipped?"

"*After*," Annabel said pointedly, setting her jaw. Taking no note of her reply, the man retrieved a heavy tin coffeepot and a small cotton sack. Pulling the lid off of a large can he scooped a handful of beans into the sack and tied it off before setting it into the coffeepot with a clunk.

"Do an old man a favor and go out to pump some water for me. The pump's out back," he said, kicking a metal bucket to Annabel as he spoke. It was less of a request and more of a command, which the girl resented. But a water pump meant a drink, and coffee soon after, so she obliged the odd old hermit.

She stepped outside to see the marshal's horse staring into the dirt, watching a field mouse nibble away at some shrunken timothy. Watchful black eyes stared at the tiny creature with what Annabel could only envision as malice. Trying to ignore the horse, she continued walking out behind the cabin to an old water pump. She cranked as hard as she could over a dozen times before the thing finally yielded cold water. She put her head under the spigot and shivered as the cold water hit her hair and the back of her neck, and drank deeply for a few pumps, gulping down the icy and metallic tasting water. After drinking her fill, she set to topping off the bucket before heading back inside.

The horse was still staring at the mouse. Annabel walked past it, paying the creature little mind until it suddenly darted its head downwards towards the ground, lifting the mouse into the air with its teeth. A horrible crunching sound followed as the black steed devoured the creature, its powerful teeth crushing bones and all before it swallowed the broken and bloody mass. It almost made Annabel sick. She had never seen a horse eat flesh before, and it made her shiver far worse than the cold water soaked into her hair, her shaking causing her to spill water from the bucket held in her shaking hands. She hurried back into the cabin, eager to be away from the thing, which seemed to be relishing its meal.

The thin man was squatting beside the fire with the pot in hand, he took a look at her face and laughed.

"You look paler than yesterday's moon. Water too cold for a bath, is it?"

"That horse just ate a mouse," she said, still shaken but coming back down, handing the bucket to the man.

"Horses don't eat mice," he said gruffly, taking the bucket and pouring a fair measure of water into the coffeepot before setting it directly onto the fire.

"I know what I saw old-timer."

"I know what I *said* missy," he replied with venom, "You bite all of your hosts that offer you sanctuary like this?"

"I'm sorry, mister," Annabel said, realizing how she must appear to the stranger, "We've been beset with troubles this past day and it weighs heavily on me."

The man spit into the fire. His face bore deep lines that had been drawn by troubles of his own over many years. He knew what the girl meant, and that she meant no harm by her tone.

"Don't worry about it, no offense is taken by it. I have some cornmeal left from the trading-man. I'll fix us some quick meal cakes. I haven't had company in a long time out here, you can tell me what you're doing out this way while we breakfast."

After a while, the coffeepot began to steam loudly, and the thin man withdrew if from the fire with his hook and set it on the table. He busied himself at another cabinet, grabbing two tin cups and plates before setting them upon the table. Annabel poured a scalding-hot cup of coffee for herself and watched the man mix the remaining water and a handful cornmeal into a paste. He then set a heavy skillet into the fire and threw in a lump of bacon fat that hissed and spat before he placed lumps of the cornmeal mixture into it.

Once the cakes were fried and placed onto plates, the two ate and drank in silence. Annabel ate with her fingers, as did her host. Feeling far better with something warm in her guts, Annabel withdrew her poke and rolled herself a cigarette before offering one to the thin man. She lit the smoke for him and drew on her own, sighing and allowing herself to relax.

"So, what brings you and a man with a broken arm out to this empty expanse of the territories?" he said, exhaling a thick cloud of smoke.

"We were looking for a girl who went missing from Ganndo Valley out near Emmet Mine."

96

"That was a damn fool idea," the man said with a scowl, "There's nothing but death down there. No decent folks go missing near that accursed mine."

"It wasn't her fault. I know there's something evil down there," she said. The thin man's face was drawn tight with anger, and his eyes burned with intensity. He slammed his cup onto the table and pointed menacingly at Annabel with his hook.

"If you knew you'd have stayed away. It's always been a dangerous place. It's boarded up for a reason. Cave-ins, missing surveyors, poisonous air, poisonous *things*. Warnings are plastered all over the entrance to the damn thing, and it was boarded up for a reason."

Speechless and shocked, Annabel stared at the man, whose lip was now trembling with rage. How did he know so much about the place? Then it hit her, and she recalled the warning Mr. Jeffries had given her in his office.

"You're one of the missing surveyors," she said as the realization came to her, "A group of speculators went missing years ago."

The thin man laughed, and the sound of it was cruel and cold, almost pitying. It was tinged with a disgusted irony.

"Do I look like a mining speculator to you? No surveyors or speculators have been in the Emmet Mine since it was closed after what we found down there."

"I thought you didn't find anything," Annabel said, growing uncomfortable again, her hand slowly drifting to her pistol under the table.

"If you've been down there you know that's not true," the thin man said, "And if you're referring to the old story about there being no silver down there, that's all it is. A *story*. Any real surveyor around that place could tell you based on how much galena is out there that the mine is chock-full of silver ore. We spread that story about it being a worthless proposition to keep people out."

"Who's *we*?" Annabel asked, still ready to draw the gun at a moment's notice.

"The marshals. Like him," the man said, tilting his head towards the marshal on the bed, "I'd recognize that suit anywhere. There was a time when I wore one myself and rode a black mount as he does."

"Wait, the Marshals were here before?" the sheriff asked.

"Twice before. At first when the mine opened, right after the claim was staked. Things went smoothly enough, according to the reports we were given on my trip out this way. But then people started disappearing. And worse, they would re-appear sometime later, but they came back *changed*. Back then the Marshals were new. At least, in the way they were organized. We've been around for a long, long time by different names, but when the Marshals were officially founded, things started to come together. We were just starting to get more organized. More official. Some of the first members to wear the badge were sent to investigate and found something down there. Something evil. Once they realized what the thing was doing, they buried it and came up with the story that the mine was a worthless proposition. They tried to kill it with conventional arms, but were unsuccessful, so they settled for closing the thing off until they cracked how to destroy it. A few years later they sent two of us out here to deal with the thing. To kill it. We posed as speculators when questioning the locals before we went into the mine to destroy the thing."

"You didn't do a great job. It's still down there," the sheriff said grimly, recalling the image of Rosanna, mutated and twisted into a horrible dribbling monster.

"It's not stupid," the old hermit said bitterly, "It knows better than to take decent folk. At worst it swallows a drifter every month or so. More often in the winter when they wander inside of the thing to hide from the elements. Other than that, it's outlaws and degenerates. We weren't saving anyone worth saving by chasing after the thing. But we were young. *I* was young. Young and stupid."

Sitting quietly, the man didn't reply. His expression was difficult to read, but his demeanor softened, and he seemed morose to Annabel.

"Something happened down there," she said, coming to realize that the old man's experience in the mine may not have been much different from her own.

"Look miss, I don't want to guess what happened that caused them to send another man out here to deal with it again. You want my advice, you go on and forget about it. It can't be stopped, and it can't be killed."

"That's not good enough!" Annabel yelled, standing and shaking with fury, "This thing took and twisted an innocent young girl with her whole life ahead of her. It stole her life! It's causing chaos in my territory, and I'll be damned if I don't see the thing hanged one way or another. This isn't some one-off case for me before I hop a train back east. This is my home, and I'll defend it with my bare hands if I have to."

Looking at her with tired yet compassionate eyes, the old thin man shook his head with pity.

"I have felt that fire that burns inside you right now, and I know the loss that enkindles it," he said, putting his cigarette out in the bottom of his empty coffee tin.

"I came here with another marshal named Deacon. He was as close to me as any soul on this earth. Both of us fought for what we thought was true and just. The marshals used us, they exploited our zeal for serving a righteous cause. They swallow up young lives. They didn't care for what hell they sent us into. We foolishly trusted in lead and steel to see us through. If you have seen what lurks down there at the heart of that monstrosity, you will know any mortal man is helpless against it. We tore into it with metal and fire and watched as it clung to life and shifted into more grotesque and vile forms before our very eyes. I watched it tear a man apart and turn him inside out, and I had to watch as the one person I cared for most was swallowed by the darkness itself as he fell into a chasm so deep there was no sound within it. The place swallowed him alive. Deacon died because the Marshals meddle with things that man has no right to fool with. They're just as bad as the conjurers and sorcerers they stand opposed to. Worse even."

Leathery skin was drawn tightly around his clenched jaw, the pain on his face shrinking his mouth into a razor-thin line as the man clamped his eyes shut. Annabel could only stare, holding her coffee in both hands.

"Bury it and let it pass from your mind," he said, regaining his composure and steadying his shaking hand, "With luck its memory will not scar you as it has me, and you can live a life much like what you may have lived before you knew such horrors existed."

Annabel set her cup atop the table.

"I don't know what to say."

100

"Say nothing. Know I am right," the thin man said, standing and approaching the unconscious young marshal.

"Know that the fire you spoke of that burns inside you will fade. That inner voice calling you to *purpose* and to *justice*, speaks of little more than bold words too often spoken by men who do not understand them. Trust me as I say it will fade."

The sheriff set aside her cigarette, which bore a long ashen tip itself after being neglected while the old man spoke. She set the butt into her empty cup and swallowed hard. The old and broken hermit had a point. There was nothing she could do to save Rosanna now. She had watched the marshal shoot the creature that wore the girl's body as its own, seen the bullet rip through rotting and mutated flesh that no longer resembled what she once was. Perhaps the old man was right. Studying her face, the thin man nodded and closed his eyes in pained relief.

"I am glad to know it will not take the life of one so brave as yourself, miss."

"I can't leave this thing out here," she started to say, but she failed to find how to express the fact that she knew she was beaten. This thing was bigger than her, bigger than anything she had ever known before. A kind of evil that seemed so unreal, so impossible that she felt helpless even considering going up against it again. This man had tried before knowing more about such things than even the marshal, and he himself said it was impossible to stop. He was right. Annabel hated it but knew it in her bones that he was right. All she had needed was an excuse to put this horrid affair behind her, and now that she had one, she felt small and weak for accepting it. Defeated and somewhat relieved all at once, the sheriff sighed and shook her head slowly.

"I-," Annabel searched for what to say, "I don't know my way back to the valley from here."

101

"You can follow the tree line east, it circled back around to the town on the other side. I'll take care of him," he said, looking at the marshal on the bed, "I'll see he heals up and is sent back east. No sense in young folk like him dying for nothing out here in the wilderness."

Annabel held her ground, unsure if it was safe to leave the marshal with the old man.

"I should take him back to town with me," she said. "Mr. Jeffries can tend to his wounds."

"The ride wouldn't be good for him, injured as he is," the old man reasoned, "I may not be a marshal anymore, but we look after our own."

"What about his horse?" Annabel asked. The hermit made a face when she said the word 'horse,' but he pointed outside with his good hand.

"Leave his mount, you can take my mule. She's old but sturdy. The trip back won't take more than two days, and I'll make sure you're provisioned."

With nothing else to say, the sheriff nodded in thanks. She stood and could not bear to look at the old man, feeling guilt twist around in her guts. With time she hoped to forget everything she had seen in recent days. She'd ride back to town and round up whatever explosives were left over from the old mining days and take a posse out to blow the entrances to Emmet Mine once and for all. She would leave the thing to starve beneath the earth, buried and forgotten.

Annabel turned to the door and left the old man behind with the marshal, trusting that the man would take care of one of his own. Perhaps the hermit could talk some sense into the marshal, too.

Leaving the isolated cabin without another word, Annabel awkwardly made her way outside to mount up and ride back to Ganndo Valley, alone.

Chapter X

The marshal awoke to the smell of freshly ground coffee and the rich scent of firewood after what felt like a millennium of sleep.

With a groan he rose from the cot upon which he lay and turned towards the man sitting alone at a small kitchen table cradling a tin cup of piping hot coffee. Most curiously, the marshal noted that the man had a hook for a hand.

Swallowing hard to clear his throat, which felt as cracked and dry as desert hardpan, the marshal found his voice.

"I don't suppose I could trouble you for a cup of that coffee?"

The old thin man rolled his eyes and scoffed. He handed the coffee tin to the marshal.

"You were coughing and groaning in your sleep, and since you haven't made a peep for almost two days, I reckoned you were about to come to or die. Depending on whether or not you did end up croaking, this coffee could have been for me or you. Enjoy it, son."

Looking perplexed, the marshal cautiously took the hot metal cup from the old man and drank it down, letting the nearly scalding beverage punish his throat while at the same time warming and comforting his cold guts.

"Much obliged, friend," he croaked, wincing a bit after downing the java. The old man squinted hard and poured himself a cup and gave the marshal a refill.

"Friend, huh?" the old man said with a disinterested glance at the marshal, "I suppose they're teaching you to be more polite these days, I take it?"

The marshal stared at the one-handed old timer with mounting discomfort and suspicion. His cryptic speech and strange appearance made the hackles on his neck stand up. The last thing he remembered was darkness and the smell of smoke, and the girl, Sheriff Annabel comforting him.

"Where am I?" he asked plainly, which seemed to satisfy the old man.

"My cabin outside of the woods," the man replied. He took the coffeepot and set it onto the table quietly with his hook before leaning back in an old careworn wooden chair.

"The young lady that was with you left two days ago. She went back to Ganndo Valley, on the other side of the pines. Girl came to her senses about the mess you've gotten her involved in."

Unable to do anything but stare, the marshal was left speechless. The old man had to be lying. There was no way that Anna would up and abandon him out here, let alone abandon pursuing and destroying the thing that had preyed on her town. The marshal could not believe it.

Without elaborating further, the old man sipped his coffee and rocked back and forth in his creaking chair, as if he were waiting for something. His mind still tumbling around his current circumstances, the marshal could not bring himself to form a coherent sentence.

"Don't give me that look," the thin old man said, "You know better than to involve the locals when on a case. It always, *always* turns out sour. Count yourself lucky she wasn't killed."

The old man had him made as a marshal. He'd been found out and was in a stranger's home, drinking his coffee which might even be poisoned. The cup tilted in the marshal's hand, dripping coffee onto the mattress beneath him.

"You're spilling your bean juice there, partner."

"Who are you and what have you done with Anna?" the marshal asked, his uninjured hand slowly drifting to the knife in his boot.

"For a marshal, you're awfully slow partner. And you make a try for that knife in your boot you'd better be faster than I am," the old man said, pulling up the leg of his trousers to reveal his own knife, which was clearly older while being identical to the marshal's.

In an instant, the marshal realized what was happening and stopped trying to reach his knife.

"*You*? You're a marshal?"

"I *was*. The tax on a man's soul for doing the kind of work was too high for me. Too high for any man. Call me what you like, I've never brokered on having to need a real name again, especially out here."

The marshal's eyes fell to the hook the man wore.

"What are you doing out here? And I'll ask again, where is the sheriff?"

106

"The sheriff huh? A moment ago, she was 'Anna,'" he said with a slight smile, "Marshal Hook was my old handle back when I rode with the company. Does no good just to call each other 'marshal,' like schoolboys with secret names."

"Now *that* I cannot sanction," the marshal stuttered in denial, "I cannot believe that you're *the* genuine Marshal Hook. The man was a hero. He rode with Marshal Deacon against the Pickety Witch and put her into the ground. You can't be him."

"What would you know about it?" Hook quipped with irritation, visibly recoiling at the mention of Deacon's name, "The business with the Pickety Witch was done before you were even born. As for the sheriff I sent her back to town on my mule. The girl is level-headed enough to know when she's licked. Some things man just weren't meant to tangle with. I'd suspect she might actually follow my advice to bury the damn thing and seal up that old mine."

"Because that worked so well before, right?" the marshal asked with dark sarcasm, "It's spreading its roots down there. People as far east as Mantis City have been taken and twisted by it. It is *growing* down there. And if we ignore it, the creature could get big enough to consume the entire continent if left unchecked."

"*If left unchecked*," Hook mocked, "That rhetoric doesn't resonate so well with a man who knows what it really means. Unchecked by whom? You? A bunch of boys with mustaches and girls with tight braids wearing the same grey suit, trained and prepared for something you cannot truly prepare for? No, boy. There is an inevitability to these things. Despite his advances in science and medicine and war, man cannot control or confront these things that are older and more powerful than he. Accept it. Believe it. Enjoy the life you've been given and accept that there

107

are things out there that you cannot change. Leave the thing be. One girl among a sea of villains and killers over the last decade is nothing to bemoan. Any hazards have acceptable losses, be they supernatural or just plain bad luck."

"So that's why you've given up," the marshal said after a pause, "*Acceptable losses.* How enlightened."

Stepping away from the cot and dusting off his suit jacket, the marshal stretched and tested his joints. His left arm was in bad shape, but his wound was bound, and he was luckily right-handed. He felt strong enough anyway. Old Hook's speech about surrender and acceptance had awoken a defiant beast within him.

"One innocent life is enough for me to at least try to stop this thing. Whether or not I am doomed to fail doesn't enter into my thinking," the young marshal said with a wide and bold smile, his sense of purpose restored and stronger than ever.

"They won't mourn you when you fall," Hook said, "Better men than you have died in their service. All they have to show for it is a name etched on that ugly wall of black marble and move on to the next one. The company does not care for you, or for the toll they are asking you to pay on mankind's behalf."

"I suppose I'll pay that bill when it's due, then," the marshal said heading to the door. Hook's face was a lined mask of bitterness coupled with pity and sorrow. The man felt devastated to see a young man that reminded him so much of Deacon about to head to his death. The marshal seemed unperturbed by this and had found the spring in his step again. He turned to the old tired ex-marshal and gave the man a chipper salute.

"You enjoy yourself with the life you've been given, correction, that you have *chosen.* I hope you find comfort in your acceptance and wisdom that is clearly far beyond my understanding. Farewell Mr. Hook."

Not a moment later, the marshal was out the door and in the saddle upon his ebon steed, riding back out east to Ganndo Valley, leaving old Marshal Hook in his nearly empty cabin, alone.

Field of green and faded gold raced past the marshal as he rode across the wide open plain. His mount sped forward like a black bolt of lightning across the range, its wild mane fluttering in the wind.

It would be difficult to convince Sheriff Annabel to help him again, and he wondered if it was even the right thing to do to ask for her aid. While in his heart he knew the things that Hook had said back at the cabin were little more than the defeated musings of a tired and weary man, there were kernels of truth mired in his words.

Involving Annabel in this business may have been rash, or even wrong to do, but he had little choice. She saw what had happened to the men in her cell and knew that someone or something meant her people harm. It just felt wrong to the marshal to shut her out, to keep her blind to what was happening. All he could do now was hope that he had done the right thing, and that approaching her once more to bring her back into the thick of things was the right thing as well.

As he rode on, he realized that the journey would not be completed in a day, and silently cursed himself for not asking Hook for a bit of coffee before verbally lambasting the man. The marshal put his head down and rode on back to the valley.

Chapter XI

Annabel had arrived in town late in the evening of her second day's ride. She had lost time going back to retrieve her horse, *Blunderbuss* from the entrance to the pines where he had been left tied to a tree. The old stallion looked at her with tired eyes, completely unaware that his master had seen and faced trials and terrors deep beneath the earth mere days before. He had almost completely grazed all the grass around him and looked glad to be untethered and moving again. Both she and the horse could do with a bowl of hot oatmeal and a long night's rest. She held the reigns of the mule she had rode in one hand, and rode *Blunderbuss* back to town, leading the mule alongside her.

As she passed the large wooden fence of Mr. Abernathy's property, the sheriff felt exhaustion truly set in. She was tired and saddle-sore. The trip back had been a quiet and sullen affair, and she found herself missing the odd banter from the marshal on the trail. She hoped he was alright in the old hermit's care out on the plains. If she did see the man again, she was not sure she could bring herself to give him anything more than a brief goodbye as he would no doubt head for the train station and for home.

Beneath the starlit sky, the town looked the same way Annabel felt. Dark and quiet, only partly alive. A few errant lights from candles or lanterns flickering within people's homes gave her any indication that anyone was awake at all.

She returned her horse to the stables and put the old man's mule in the stall where the marshal's beast was kept. She'd have to pay to board the creature until she could return it to the old hermit's cabin.

Once the animals were put to their stalls and bedded, she made her way over to the *Rye in the Sky*. A harmonica played from within, gently and softly. It was late even for the gamblers, and Annabel could only hope they stayed open long enough for her to get one good drink.

Her boots thumped heavily on the worn floorboards as she strode across the porch and through the swing doors, nodding to young Colm who stood at the door in front of the weapon's box. The kid looked alert as she entered, no doubt recalling the action that took place the last time she had been in the saloon.

"Evening Sheriff!" he drawled with a nervous smile.

"Howdy Colm. Nobody's in trouble, just here for a drink."

The boy looked disappointed but relieved and let her pass with her iron. She stopped for a moment. It was not her revolver in the holster at her side, but rather the marshal's. She shook her head. The less she thought of him, the better. The old man was right, if would be best to leave the marshal and his kind alone. She'd return the pistol to his office by post tomorrow and set out with a crew to seal up the mine and any holes out in the rock near the pines. After that, the entire mess would be behind her.

She drifted to the bar and sat upon a creaking polished wooden stool and rested her elbows on the counter. Mr. Abernathy quickly stowed the sliver of wood he had been using to pick his teeth and ran his fingers through his hair to tidy it.

"Good evening, Sheriff, what can I get you?"

"A whiskey if you please, Jonas."

Without looking, the barkeep collected the bottle and glass in one hand, set down the glass, and poured the whiskey without looking, performing the action he had done thousands of times without a thought. Annabel slid an unevenly folded bill across the smooth wooden bar top and lifted the glass of whiskey. It felt impossibly heavy in her weary hand.

"Anything in particular you're looking to burn away with this?" he asked, something else he had also practiced before, the art of conversation.

"Hell, I don't know," Annabel said, pressing her thumb and forefinger on the bridge of her nose. She then took up her glass and emptied it, the spiced honey taste catching in her throat and nostrils almost made her cough.

The barkeep waited, still giving her his attention but busying himself with stacking glasses. If she felt like talking, it would be soon. If not, he'd move on to check in with Wilson and Leeroy, who had been playing chess for a few hours. The game had been an enjoyable and civil one, and the barman figured he could get each of them at least one more drink before someone muttered checkmate.

"Am I a good sheriff, Jonas?" she asked, too tired to care how the question sounded. Old Bill choked on his harmonica for a moment before starting back up again. The barman looked at the young lady for a moment with his mouth agape, uncertain how to answer her. He felt unprepared and overwhelmed all at one and sputtered a bit before trying to ground himself enough to reply.

"Well shoot. Of course, you're a good sheriff. Everybody knows that," he said, meaning every word but struggling not to sound saccharine, "You give folks an honest shake and come down hard when you need to, not too hard mind but, you know…tarnation you know what I mean. Why are you asking me a question like that?"

Annabel looked over her glass sullenly as Jonas, uncertain what to do, refilled it. She downed the amber whiskey as soon as he had finished pouring, and he automatically topped it off again.

"I feel like I'm being tested," she said slowly, watching the lamplight reflected in the curvature of the glass, "It has always been easy for me to know what was right or wrong, to know that I could face adversity and make a call firmly in the right. I *knew*, without a single doubt, what was just. But now, after everything that has happened since I shot that man standing right here, where I am sitting right now, I haven't been sure."

Jonas Abernathy said nothing. He fumbled with a glass he held before setting it down beside his stack, unable to balance it properly. He opened his mouth to speak, only to close it again after realizing he had nothing to say.

From behind her, Annabel heard the doors swing open and Colm gasp quietly. In her glass that reflected the room, she could see a dark shape approaching the bar. A man in a dark suit. For a moment, her guts tightened and fluttered at the thought of having to speak with the marshal, and to tell him she would no longer be assisting his investigation. She wasn't sure she could muster the courage to ask him to leave town, exhausted and drunk and emotionally drained.

Instead of the marshal sitting beside her, Annabel was surprised to see a stranger in a worn out and dirty black suit sit beside her. The man reeked of chemicals and even Jonas stepped away from the stranger, despite being accustomed to the smell of men who had worked long days under the hot sun at his bar in the summertime. Long greasy hair hung down to the lapels of the man's jacket, and his skin was pale and almost grey in the dim lantern light.

"Howdy there, barman," the stranger said with a heavy, musty voice, "How about some whiskey for me and my companions?"

Without warning, one of the stranger's friends reached across the bar and took the bottle of whiskey Jonas was holding and wrenched it out of his hands. Annabel moved to stand but quickly gauged that she was outnumbered. She slowly tried to move her hand to the pistol at her side but was far too drunk and clumsy. The man on the stool beside her clucked his tongue and wagged a finger.

"Oh no Miss Sheriff. None of that here, now. We're all friends enjoying a drink here, right partner?" he said to the barman with a savage yellow-toothed grin. The man's gums were deep scarlet black, and Annabel at once realized how grave the situation had become. Jonas eyed Annabel and signaled with a glance under the counter, where he had a shotgun stowed away. She shook her head no. They were outnumbered, and if these men were armed, they had not left their weapons with Colm.

Annabel forgot herself as she remembered Colm was standing by the door, and turned in her stool, horrified to see that a skinny short man in a duster had a lever action rifle leveled and pointed at the young man. Colm himself had a revolver in his hands, but had drawn too late, and the barrel of his gun pointed uselessly at the ground as he had frozen mid-draw.

Heavy hands clapped onto her aching shoulders and forced her down onto the stool, turning her to face the long-haired stranger beside her. He chuckled and snorted, hocking up a wad of snot and spitting it into the spittoon beside the bar with a loud clang.

"I like you ma'am. You've got guts," he said, taking the bottle from one of his associates. He raised it to his lips and took a mammoth drink before continuing, "I'd hate to add another violent event to this establishment's storied history tonight, so me and mine are willing to make you a *deal*."

Annabel scowled at the man, her hateful gaze boring into the man's own ruddy green eyes. He snickered.

"We don't want *you*. We want the other stranger. The government man. The spook. He's about Bart's height," he jerked a thumb to the man threatening Colm, "Black mustache, grey suit, poor taste in horseflesh. You give him to us, and we'll all quietly slink back to where we come from without another peep. He's standing in the way of a unification unlike any this worthless world has ever seen."

Annabel's lips tightened and her brow furrowed. These were men from the mine, she just knew it. They had followed her here, somehow, or they simply knew to check the only town close enough to ride to on horseback. Either way, just by being here they were putting everyone in danger.

"Strong and silent, isn't she?" the man asked Jonas with a measured smile, who was trying to stand still and breathe quietly. The man reached across the table and brushed a few crumbs off of the barman's shirt.

Swiftly and violently, the man grabbed Jonas' tie and pulled his head onto the bar with a crash, and he hoisted the whiskey jug high into the air, sloshing alcohol all over himself, Annabel, and

Jonas. His face was even paler, granite-grey in the dim light and his features were a mask of insanity and malice

"I am not a patient man, lady!" he shouted, standing and kicking his stool out from under him and menacing the barman, "I'll split his blasted head open if you don't say something! Say it! Where's the spook!?"

"I don't know!" Annabel screamed, "We went separate ways after we got out of the mine!"

"Liar!" the creep smashed the bottle on the bar inches from Mr. Abernathy's face, sending glass and whiskey everywhere. He drew a blued revolver from his waist and shoved the barrel against Abernathy's temple, cramming it up against the top of the man's ear. He cocked the hammer and stared at Annabel, his pupils shaking as they glanced back and forth across her face.

"You lie to me and I *will* kill him! Where's the marshal!?"

"I don't know," the sheriff said, trying to keep her voice as calm and even as possible, "We split up in the pines. I don't know."

The man licked his lips like a monitor lizard, staring her down, searching her face for any sign of deception. Near the door, the man named Bart cleared his throat.

"Slate, I think she may be telling the truth. Only one horde rode out of them woods when I was on watch. Marley was with me, we've seen only one horse, boss."

Catching himself and regaining a small measure of his wicked composure, the man with the gun, Slate, eased the hammer down. Jonas sighed with relief, still terrified but breathing again. Slate turned his gaze back to Annabel.

"Which way did he go? And if you say 'I don't know' one more time I'll stove this pig's head in."

"He went north," Annabel lied, staring unblinking into the reeking man's face.

"Anything of merit up there, boys?" he asked his companions.

"Naw, boss," the one said who was holding the sheriff down, "Just the train station, which we know is safe, and that's a fair ride from here. If he's heading back east, he'd have to go there. No way a man on horseback is getting past the mountain range the train tunnels through."

"Alright. How many of the townsfolk do we have already up at the hotel?" he asked. Annabel paled with horror, recalling all of the dazed and half-asleep movements of the townsfolk over recent days. They had all been touched by this parasitic fever.

"Near half,"

"Not good enough to take it all yet, then," the slender man muttered hatefully, "Not enough to pull back that wall of ore and stone…"

Slate released the barman's tie and holstered his pistol, licking spilled whiskey off the back of his hand.

"Count yourself very lucky, Sheriff. You'll have dozens of eagle-eyed friends of yours, now also friends of *mine* watching over you for the next few days. The ruckus you started down in the mine has shifted things a bit. Put us on a tighter timetable if you get my meaning. Things move fast when you're expanding business, don't they? You *do* get my meaning, don't you sweetheart?"

Annabel shot him a look more hateful than any she had worn in her entire lifetime. For a moment, the outlaw looked genuinely frightened before he remembered that he had the young lady outnumbered.

"The way I figure it, you've got only a couple of days before you become a part of a greater whole, missy," he sneered, "Trust me when I say, once you are joined with us you'll be glad for it. Something is coming. Something far worse than us!"

The bandit whistled, circling an arm in the air. The rest of the gang left slowly, all but the man holding down Annabel, the man holding up Colm, Bart, and Slate himself.

"I'll be watching you personally to make sure you don't do anything stupid, Sheriff. You and your pals are going to stay right here in this lovely saloon for a day or two, with your friends and neighbors looking out for you."

The man holding her shoulders released her, and both he and Slate headed towards the door with their back to her. Unable to do anything without risking Colm's life, she waited until they were out the door, and watched Bart back away with Colm still in the sights of his rifle until they were out of view.

Jonas slumped against the back wall of the bar, causing the bottles to rattle and jangle musically together. In the corner, Old Bill had his harmonica clutched in both hands, looking like an angry child cradling a toy. Both Wilson and Leeroy stared at Annabel, heedless of the remaining chess pieces laying in front of them, knocked to the ground by startled hands.

Getting to her shaking feet, Annabel stood up slowly, drawing the marshal's pistol with a smooth and even motion. Jonas' eyes lit up with horror, and he hissed in a loud whisper.

118

"No! Are you crazy, girl? Going up against them all alone, they'd kill you for sure!"

"I can't sit in here and wait while a gang of outlaws and buffoons try to take control of my town," she replied, "Whether or not they've thrown in with some penny dreadful thing from Emmet Mine."

Jonas, not understanding the last thing she said, grabbed her by the wrist.

"Sheriff, you can't go out there, you can barely stand!"

"Standing or not, my trigger finger works just fine."

Leeroy stood up and approached the young woman, standing in front of her. His tired face was still flushed with fear, but he wore an expression of pleading sincerity.

"Anna, listen to Mr. Abernathy. We need to think this through, and you need rest and likely a bite to eat before we make our move."

From the table behind Leeroy, Wilson nodded in agreement. At the door, Colm was still reeling from the encounter, his slim frame wavering with fear as he supported himself on the empty gunrack behind him. Annabel wavered for a moment before half-collapsing back into her stool, her borrowed pistol feeling incredibly heavy in her right hand.

"We can't let them take it, Jonas," she said quietly, her composure slipping, coming undone at the seams, "What cruel intentions they have planned for us are the very terrors of the earth."

"Then I reckon we'll have to stop them," the portly barman said. Annabel looked at him and chuckled weakly.

119

"You?"

"Well shoot," he said, slightly offended, "I know I've gotten wider as time has gone on but I'm still a fair shot with the scattergun. Colm over yonder has his pistol, and Old Bill has his .45 stashed away someplace. We could gather a few folks to deputize and requisition some arms from Duncan's store. He said a dozen friends. We can gather a posse near that size."

Leeroy seemed agreeable with the prospect, as did Old Bill, bolstered by what the barman proposed. Annabel shook her head, and all four men in the bar lost the hopeful glint in their eyes.

"*Dozens*," she interjected, "As in, plural. We can't know how many mad devotees he has with him. And I've seen you shoot. Unless the whole town was behind you and that shotgun I'd be worried as all get-out. Lastly, we'd have to get out to even warn somebody, and I doubt we can just sneak out of here."

The sheriff neglected to add that she could not risk asking townsfolk for help when they may be infected and a part of this horrible colony of creatures. She holstered the weapon she held with great effort and slumped down to rest her forearms on the bar again.

"You are right about me being dog-tired, Jonas," she admitted, "And we may have a chance. You and Leeroy take an inventory of how many shells we've got for that shotgun under the counter there. Colm, I want to know how many rounds and arms you have in that cage and counter over yonder. Old Bill and Wilson can get to pulling strips of cloth for me. Thin ones, like a necktie. From anything but the curtains mind you, we'll need those."

Leeroy and Wilson each gave a nod, while Old Bill remained silent, the corner of his mouth moving slightly to convey his agreement. Jonas looked on board with the idea but seemed confused about one singular aspect.

"What are *you* going to do, Sheriff?"

"I'm going to get some shut eye before we burn those parasites out of our town."

Chapter XII

Riding for over a day before stopping, the marshal finally allowed himself a brief rest before he continued on. The sun had retreated from the horizon hours ago, and night had fallen heavily over the open field upon which he now rested, setting down to make camp on the open frontier.

He made a small camp, with a tiny fire in a pit no larger than his first, with little more than stubborn grasses and a few twigs for the flames to nibble on. The nights on the plain were cold, but he'd make do. The man in grey was trained to make do.

His jet-black mount lay on the ground nearby, with his great head and glinting obsidian eyes gazing at the tiny flame. The orange shape danced in the dark orbs as a haunting reflection that the marshal knew not to look at for too long.

With a groan he reached for his saddlebags with his injured left arm. It was still not healed yet, and in his routine of making camp he had almost forgotten his injury.

Instead he pulled the bag open with his right hand and reached into the seemingly empty bag.

His fingers pulled at a dummy thread on the inside to open the hidden flap at the bottom of the tooled leather, where his supplies were kept hidden. The hidden compartment kept bandits, nosy stablemasters, and unfriendly local law from robbing him on the trail. Carefully withdrawing a few orange shotgun shells, he busied himself with reloading his lever-action shotgun.

It was heavy and unwieldly, the old cast iron thing, and reloading it was tiresome work to do one-handed. The beast beside him hissed in shuddering notes, almost like mocking laughter, ridiculing the marshal. The man smiled wryly.

"I'd like to see you try it."

The creature did not reply.

After carefully loading the thing he returned it to the holster on the saddle and checked his other gear. The derringer in his boot was still there, loaded and ready with its single shot, as were the extra cartridges for it, stored in his bootheel. Not that it would be much use in a pinch anyway, his left hand couldn't draw it, injured as it was.

He unfastened a measure of leather from one of his stirrups and fashioned himself a crude sling to cradle his injured arm. The contraption wasn't very comfortable on his shoulder but took the weight and strain off of the damaged limb.

Lastly, he replaced the missing cartridges in his gun belt, putting the empty brass back into the saddlebag before withdrawing a bite of jerky from within. He closed up the flap and pulled the dummy thread tight as he chewed. This night, with the ritual of making camp and checking his equipment was like so many other nights he had spent in countless other places. But unlike those nights, his focus was split. Confused.

His thoughts were on his task, of course. Knowing that if the sheriff refused to help him confront and destroy the monster in the mine, he would have to do so alone. His thoughts were also on the sheriff herself, in a dangerous way. She had offered him a way out, and the marshal truly didn't know if he even wanted one. The work he did with the Marshals was everything to him. His very identity was rooted in his station. Yet the prospect of having a chance to act as law for a nice, small town with such comforts was tempting. For the first time in his career, the two-headed serpent of doubt slithered its way into his chest and made itself at home there.

What Hook had said muddled everything. Clearly coming from a bitter and misguided place, but with some bits of sense hidden within. The marshal wondered what happened to the man to twist him against the Marshals so much. He could not imagine what would drive someone to lie down and give up in that way. While it did happen, it rarely was a seasoned and historied veteran who gave up the life. Marshals that quit were as green as they come, and usually the first taste of the dark was what made a person decide to stay in the shadows and face them head-on, or to run screaming back into the comfort of ignorance. The marshal had chosen the former. Once his eyes were opened to this world of secrets and magic, he had no wish to ever turn back. At least, not at first. Now, in this place, he wasn't so sure.

He cursed Hook as he tended to his fire. Everything the old hermit had said made a cruel kind of sense to the marshal, and he disliked the thought that the old man was right.

What made it worse is that the old ex-marshal had a point about not involving outsiders in office business, he also had a point about letting people feel safe in their ignorance. Telling Annabel about the nature of the disappearances in her town was perhaps a grave error in the marshal's judgement. And involving her had made it more complicated for himself as well, now that he was developing a fondness for the woman.

He didn't want Annabel to be looking over her shoulder for the rest of her life, expecting some terror or another to be lurking there. On the other hand, he wondered what kind of life he might have if he did follow the old man's advice and gave it all up.

Maybe she was right. Maybe he could have a life with her. He buried his face in his hands and groaned. He was thinking in circles.

From the darkness, his mount cackled wickedly again, as if sensing his thoughts. He looked to the monster of a steed and grimaced while looking to the stars.

"I know it's nonsense," he said to the beast, "But a man wonders about what shape his life can take. I'm at a sort of crossroads here, friend."

The monstrous mount beside him sneered. In the dwindling twilight it looked like nothing more than a black malevolent shape, rather than a living thing. The marshal grinned.

"I guess that makes you the devil, doesn't it?"

Still silent, the creature laid its head upon the ground and became as still as a tombstone.

For whatever it was worth, he felt firmly in the right of his current situation here. Whether or not he continued work in the Marshal's service after this withstanding, he had a job to do here, and would be damned if he didn't see it through to the end.

The marshal laid down beside his tiny fire and tried to grasp at that elusive entity named sleep.

125

He awoke to the smell of bacon and eggs, and to the gentle sound of sizzling and popping fat over a fire. He sat upright abruptly, his vision still clouded by dream-cotton. His broken arm protested loudly as he leaned on it, and he almost fell into the dirt again before catching himself with his right hand.

"I'd wager they aren't teaching you how to set watch properly anymore either," a voice said from beside him. His eyes adjusted to the bright morning sunlight and he was shocked to see old Hook squatting next to his fire, which appeared to have grown larger overnight. The old man held a skillet over the flame, crowded with eggs and strips of thick cut bacon. He used his hook to push the charcoal around beneath the skillet, carefully controlling the heat. Buried in the coals beside the skillet was a metal carafe of coffee, which was a beautiful sight to the young marshal.

Behind the old man was a horse so old it looked to the marshal like it was taxidermized. The word "nag," was almost too good for the sorry thing, but the marshal was relieved it was just a horse, unlike his own beast of burden. He could not begin to imagine what one of his own mount's breed would be like after living wild for so long. To hear the truth of it, the black steeds of the marshals only became more cruel with age.

"My second here would have woken me if there were trouble," the marshal said, rubbing his tired eyes. His mount snickered darkly with its mouth full of uncooked bacon.

"Best not to rely on such things," Hook said. The skillet he held he moved off of the flame, and slid half of its contents onto a chipped tin plate. Both the plate and a small fork were passed to the marshal. The old man poured two cups of steaming hot coffee and set them on the ground away from the campfire.

"You followed me," he said, shoveling his breakfast into his mouth with his fork. There truly was something magical about meals on the trail. Somehow, they always seemed to be far more satisfying than they had any business to be. The marshal ate like an animal while Hook served himself.

Hook was quiet, eating his breakfast with more tact than the marshal seemed capable of mustering, as hungry as he was. A tired look of regret was laid over the old ex-marshal like a heavy cloak.

"What you said back in the cabin got under my skin," he said, uncomfortable with talking so much. Hook had spoken more in the last two days than he had for many years since his terrible encounter with the being that lived deep below the earth and stone of Emmet Mine. The marshal smirked, his mustache flecked with egg yolk before he wiped his mouth off with his handkerchief.

"Convincing, wasn't it?"

"Bring down that ego of yours, kid," Hook said, "Blame the sentimentality that old age and isolation have burdened me with. What you said reminded me of something my partner said long ago…"

"You're talking about Marshal Deacon, aren't you?" the marshal asked. Hook paused and lowered his cutlery. The old man licked his lips and took a deep breath.

"Deacon was an honest soul. It's only because of my own cowardice that he was lost down there all those years ago. It should have been me. If Deacon hadn't… Had he been in my place, he would have had the guts to finish it back then. If what you say is true, and it's taking people from town, something *has* changed. It has to be stopped."

The marshal set his plate aside, picked up his coffee, with his elbows resting on his knees.

"So, what then?" he asked, "You, me, and the sheriff up against this thing, is that right?"

"No, boy," Hook replied dismissively, "Just the two of us. We go down there and take care of it ourselves. No locals. Just two men who won't be missed."

"Grim."

"*Honest*," Hook retorted, "Don't think for a moment that the marshal's office will care one bit about your fate before sending someone else to clean up your mess. And despite what thoughts you may entertain about Sheriff Annabel lamenting your loss, remember that she left you alone with me. If she never sees you again, she likely won't question it at all."

Uncertainty fell upon the marshal's shoulders. Should he try and fail to destroy the creature that stole that girl's life down in the mine, he felt chilled by the thought that the sheriff would not know his fate. On the other hand, he knew perhaps it would be best not to bring it up to her again. Just thinking about her made him feel sick inside. It wasn't like him to get wrapped up with a local, but he had never met anyone like Sheriff Annabel before in his life. She was special. Hook looked at the marshal and cleared his throat loudly to shake the man from his thoughts.

"Leave her out of it, son," he warned the marshal. "You're not the first one to wear the gray and meet someone on a case. Whatever you're feeling for the girl is not love. It's fear and adrenaline and dire circumstances."

"I'm not an idiot Hook," the marshal grumbled. "This isn't my first case, and I'm not making eyes at the locals for kicks. I really *understand* this woman. She... she offered me an out. An out from this life I've chosen. She asked me to stay on with her out here in this beautiful place. Working as local law, getting fat

128

on country cooking and fine spirits. It's a dream I didn't know I had, and I find myself actually considering it."

"Hog spit," Hook said, "I *know* you. I've known dozens of men and women like you over decades with the Marshals. The gray and black is who you *are*. There's no separating yourself from it. You will die in that suit, or one just like it, and when it's your time to go I'm sure you won't have a single regret about it."

The marshal's gaze returned to the fire after lingering on Hook for a moment. His fear was that the man was right. That there was nothing more to himself than the mustache and the suit. He scratched at his chin and took a deep breath while Hook watched him with frustration.

"Tarnation, kid. If you really aim to live and die like an honest man, then set down to stay here when we're finished. Right now is no time to be mulling over some nonsense plans for the future when there's dark work to be done. Focus and get your head back to the task at hand. We need an accounting of what arms and equipment we've got to handle the beast in the mine."

Looking at his own battered rifle in its black leather saddle holster, the marshal wondered if it would be enough. He then remembered he had lost his pistol.

"We're going to need more than one Firebrand and a sawed-off to deal with it," he said, "There's a gunsmith in Ganndo. We should at least ride over to supply ourselves. Maybe get some dynamite while we're at it if they've got any. All I have left is my rifle, which I cannot fire one-handed."

Mulling it over far longer than was comfortable for the marshal, Hook nodded as slow as molasses in agreement. He sipped his coffee thoughtfully.

"I suppose that is a fair point," he said, "Although most conventional arms aren't of much use, unless you're gunning down folks that the thing has infected. And forget killing it with dynamite. All you'll do is spread the thing around in a million pieces. We need to destroy *the heart* of the creature. We can't leave nothing left of it. Barring that, we seal the mine and make damned sure it can't infect anyone else."

Pulling the blackened cast-iron rifle from the saddle, the marshal handed it to Hook.

"They have these in your time with the Marshals?" the younger man asked. Old Hook took the weapon from the marshal and looked it over.

"Heavy piece of work," he murmured while examining it, "We had something similar back then, but not with a lever action. They could never figure how to get the block to cycle with the metal being so heavy. How many rounds?"

"Five. But you can't fire it more than once or twice at most in a real firefight. The residue from the shells coats the barrel in a whole mess of noxious, flammable chemicals. They explode if fired too often between cleaning. Not to mention, even the black iron gets hot enough to scorch a man's hands after two pulls on it."

"*That* I do remember," Hook said, looking at the metal implement that had replaced one of his own hands, "How many shells left?"

The marshal withdrew three orange shells from his coat pocket. Hook grunted in dissatisfaction.

"They aren't easy to make," the marshal admitted, "I had a full load of them when I rode out to the valley, with one full reload of spares. Fired two already, reloaded two spares."

Hook looked at the sawed-off shotgun in his own nag's saddle holster, the bright white steel barrel of the thing peeking out over the leather and shining in the sunlight. The marshal noticed the weapon and pointed at it with his fork.

"What is it?" the young marshal asked.

"Helspitter." Hook replied.

The marshal coughed and choked on his coffee.

"I thought they were all melted down," he said, recalling hearing stories about the infamously dangerous weapons. According to reports from the quartermaster's office, Helspitters more often killed the men using them than their intended target. They were made with alchemy, which was something no longer taught to the marshals, and only vaguely understood by those who specialized in it. Even then, the practice was dangerous and fraught with peril.

"I guess the letter asking me to return mine was lost in the post," Hook said with sarcasm, "I've only got two of the original shells it uses left. It takes plain 12-gauge shells as well, which is all I've used for many years."

He produced two shells from a pouch on his cracked leather belt, both with bright silver blasting caps and faded teal blue wax for the shell. Small and unassuming, their mediocre appearance made them look all the more dangerous and mysterious to the marshal. The young man was very familiar with the deceiving look some of their more hazardous equipment bore. He wondered if Hook felt the same way about it. The old man's palm was quivering.   He locked eyes with the marshal and Hook's expression became sharp and angry.

"Don't look at me like that you little spit," he said angrily, clenching the shells in his fist.

"I'm sorry, Hook."

Sighing heavily, the old man opened his fist and carefully returned the shells to his belt.

"I'm sorry, I've never been good at this part of things. Talking it through, I mean.   That was Deacon's department of expertise. The man could spin a yarn into solid gold, and at cards he played poker so mean I'd reckon the devil himself wouldn't sit opposite the man. He had an extrasensory perception for things. He could see the big picture. He would have ended this and in doing so would have saved that girl long before she was ever born."

Unwilling to interrupt, the marshal waited as the old man unburdened himself of the guilt he had buried deep inside for what seemed like a lifetime.

"We fought our way through the mine, killed maybe a dozen men it had infected, a bandit gang called the Coffin Thumpers or something inane like that.   We delved deep into the core of the mine where it had been blasted open with dynamite and confronted the heart of the creature. I had the Helspitter in my hand. The very one that now rests in that busted up old saddle yonder. I leveled it at the thing, and it was wearing the face of a kid. A little boy, no older than five. His cheeks were red and tear-stained, and it looked...*He* looked so lost and afraid. I couldn't do it. *I couldn't do it.*"

"That hesitation and loss of nerve gave it time to bring the rest of its thralls bearing down on us. Deacon didn't make it. It cost

132

me my life too, in a way. He...the kid, was beyond saving and I *knew* it. But deep down, that stupid, soft, human part of me just couldn't do it. I left the mine and sealed off the original entrance and I damned him. I damned us all."

Dumbstruck with horror and sadness, the marshal was at a loss for what to say to comfort the old man. He looked down at his empty coffee cup and recalled how deformed and misshapen the girl, Rosanna, has appeared in the cave. He shot her without hesitation. But to be face to face with the girl appearing as she did before she was possessed, or worse, to confront the thing wearing Annabel's face... he was unsure if he would have the courage to act either.

Neither man spoke as the fire popped and crackled. Overhead the clouds roamed on in their strange and slow migration going nowhere, and the tall grasses of the plain blew quietly in the wind.

"We ride back into town today, then," Hook said at last, standing on weary knees and throwing the dregs of his coffee onto the dying campfire.

The marshal mounted up and together the two began the remainder of the ride back to town.

Chapter XIII

The pair drew closer to the open field that spanned the distance between the town and the pines. Ganndo Valley was dark in the distance, and after riding all day both men paused to survey the land from the vantage point of a nearby hill.

"A man forgets what so many buildings look like all next to one another like that," Hook said solemnly. The marshal nodded in agreement. He could only imagine what the solitude that Hook had experienced in his self-imposed exile must have been like.

"It's a cozy slice of comfort, old man," the marshal said, "Perhaps when this thing is done you could find a home there. They have a whiskey you would not believe in that tiny little settlement."

"Folks got no use for a man like me in a place like that," Hook muttered stubbornly, "And I don't drink."

"Explains quite a bit about your character, then," the marshal quipped. Hook glared silently at the young man in gray before setting his gaze back on the trail. He leaned forward in the saddle, looking apprehensive. The marshal strained to see what the old man was looking at in the darkness.

After a moment, his vision sharpened, and the marshal saw it. Two men standing at the edge of the woods. Both were armed and without horses, just standing there as if guarding the border of the pines.

"Marshal," Hook began.

"I see them," the young lawman answered, pointing in their direction. The two men near the woods were far enough away not to see the pair of riders on the hill, watching them from afar.

Both figures in the dark stood as motionless as the pines themselves. The marshal's expression became grim. He feared they may be a part of the same company that fell upon him and the sheriff back in the mine. Wicked men that served the strange creature that lived beneath the pine forest. Both of them looked to be armed with long, high caliber rifles.

"What am I looking at, Marshal?" Hook said, confused by the sight, "What happened down there in that wretched pit? Why do these men look like they're *protecting* it?"

"The thing in Emmet Mine has been actively infecting men to serve it," the lawman replied with disgust, "They seem to be more or less in command of their faculties, but they are slaves to its alien will all the same. I think it plans to make a real effort to spread itself beyond the confines of this place."

Hook sputtered hatefully at the idea, revolted that the abomination had taken more souls into its decaying evil embrace. There was something else hidden behind his revulsion, something personal and deep that the marshal couldn't quite pin down.

"I can see why they sent you," he admitted, "In my time it only took strangers. But that nonsense about it spreading farther is ludicrous. It is trapped down there. It can't leave the mine."

"You sure?" the marshal asked.

"It *can't* leave the mine," Hook repeated himself, as if to make the statement more real. From experience, he knew the creature down below could not extract itself from its earthly prison, nor could it spread its dread infection from man to man.

"Unless you're a crack shot with a scattergun, we won't be able to hit them from here," the marshal said after a beat.

"Hmph," Hook growled, "We leave them, then. We can ride the ridge of the hill here around the town and enter from the other side."

The marshal nodded. The far side of town where old Hook was pointing was the old boot hill, the cemetery. None there to stop the two of them, save the dead, who in the marshal's experience didn't care one way or the other who passed by them.

Stalking across the hill, both the marshal and the old man's mounts carried them along the ridge. The moon overhead played tricks on the frontier, twisting the shape of grasses and trees into monstrous things. Both men rode cautiously, wise enough not to jump at shapes in the dark, while also wise enough to know not to discount them outright. From behind them, they heard a loud snapping sound, dry and lifeless.

Both men whirled in the saddle, moving in much the same way as they were trained to.

The marshal slipped from his saddle and landed beside his mount in a crouch, knowing he could not fire from the saddle in the state he was in. His open hand fell to his boot, drawing his derringer.

Still mounted, Hook leveled his Helspitter in his one good hand while bracing it with his hook and pointed it towards the sound.

Nothing was there.

"Kid, you heard it too?"

"Shh," the marshal hushed the old man, "Something is out there. I can't see it."

Both men waited another moment. The young marshal was acutely aware that if they did fire any weaponry up on the hill, the sound would carry down to the two watchmen near the pines, and to anyone else hidden within them. If they had to fight on this hill, they would have to dig in and keep it, or risk riding in the open where they could be shot.

Another crack, closer this time. Hook tensed up, and his breathing slowed.

Rising slowly from the edge of the hill was what looked to be the remains of a man. But the thing before the two lawmen was anything but human any longer.

Its body had split from the crown of its head to its pelvis, and the ribcage of the thing was splayed wide and open, with each rib moving as if it were articulated on its own. Steaming hot blood dripped viscously from the tear in its body, the inside of which was a raw and squirming mass of black and scarlet guts, lined with rows of malformed and twisted yellow teeth set into pus-ridden gums that ran up and down its severed spine and ribs. Its entire torso had become a gaping, tooth-filled maw that worked open and closed with grotesque and mechanical movements.

Frozen with disgust, the marshal could not bring his tiny derringer to bear, subconsciously believing that such a pitifully small arm would inflict no meaningful trauma to the thing.

Hook's face was also scrunched up and distorted with disgust, but he held his ground and fired the Helspitter at the monster.

Crashing thunder and a flash of flame followed the shot as old Hook put both barrels into the thing, firing the 12-gauge shells he had loaded earlier in the day.

Lead ripped through the thing, blowing away chunks of fleshy enamel-ridden tissue in a spray of sickly blood. It gurgled and bubbled, lurching forward more quickly now, still gnashing its mouths. Hook cracked open the shotgun to reload it, glancing downhill. The two watchmen had clearly heard the shot and were moving closer towards the hill.

The marshal's horse hissed at the thing and stepped away from it, turning slightly to angle the saddle it wore closer to the crouching marshal, as if to signal the man to draw the black Firebrand rifle from it.

Drawing closer, the thing began to shamble into a run. Hook fumbled a shell and loaded one more before snapping the weapon closed. The marshal strained to reach and draw the heavy black iron rifle from the saddle, and watched it slip and fall onto the ground.

The marshal's scream carried from the hill all the way down to the valley.

Chapter XIV

"Sheriff? Sheriff, you've got to wake up. Something's going on out there."

Pink early morning sunlight snuck into the saloon through the curtained windows. Flecks of dust caught mid-descent by the light sparkled idly as they floated to the ground. Annabel turned over from where she had been sleeping on the floor atop a pile of coats and a spare horse blanket someone had placed over her.

She stretched and shook her heard before standing. Every muscle ached and her joints were tight, as if the screws holding her body together had been twisted too far.

Beside her, Colm was kneeling next to a window with his pistol clutched in a white-knuckled grip. Annabel looked at him and then to the curtains that the boy had pulled away ever so slightly from the edge of the window.

Her fingers reached out to move the curtain aside, and Colm sucked his teeth loudly with fear.

"Wait!" he whispered, "Move it slowly, I don't want them to see us."

The sheriff moved the curtain aside in a careful and smooth motion and gasped at the sight that awaited her.

Broken and laying in heaps of colored shards, the two stained glass windows of the church had been smashed. Lying on the porch face-down was a torn apart book, the pages of which were now fluttering on the ground.

In the street itself, a chicken picked and scratched at the road, set free from whatever fence or coop it once called home. Annabel could see thin wisps of smoke rising from far away down the road, closer to the edge of town by the old boot hill.

Unlike most mornings, the streets themselves were utterly empty. That was the most chilling thing of all.

"Old Bill snuck out just last night to try to reach Duncan's shop to get more guns or find some help. *Reinforcements*, he said," Colm whispered, "We tried to tell him not to go, but you know how he is."

Too distraught to become angry, Annabel continued to stare outside at her hometown, which had been fundamentally changed in the span of one terrible night.

"Did he take any arms with him?" she asked numbly.

"Just his .45 he always seems to slip past me," Colm replied, a bit ashamed that he never had much luck collecting the weapon from Old Bill when he frequented the *Rye*.

Down a weapon, which could mean all the difference in Annabel's plan.

"Did you boys do what I asked you to last night?" she said, her senses slowly returning as she hesitantly let the curtain fall closed again.

Colm nodded. He led Annabel away from the window and towards the bar, where the items had been laid out. Behind the counter, Jonas was chewing on a long strip of jerky. He slid a plate of jerky and cheese to Annabel, who pushed it aside to examine the weaponry they had collected.

There was a box of fresh shells for the shotgun, the two that were loaded into it at the moment, and three more shells laid out beside that. Beside it on the counter was an old beat to hell pistol with a bore so caked with grime it looked as if it had been buried in the mud and dug up. There were five rounds loaded into it, and they looked more or less like Henry cartridges, .44 caliber. Beside the two guns were several strips torn or cut from a few cleaning rags and towels. All together the lot looked pitiful, not nearly enough to make do. Twenty-five shotgun shells, five shots for the filthy old revolver, and the marshal's weapon she carried, with maybe twelve rounds left on her gun belt.

"Is this it?" she asked in frustrated despair.

"That and the iron the kid's got on him," Jonas said with his mouth full. Colm set his gun on the counter, his hand shaking so badly the metal rattled on the wood until he let go of it.

"How many cartridges for this, Colm?"

The boy held up six fingers. Failing miserably at hiding her frustration, Annabel exhaled sharply through her nose. Colm looked as sorry as a kicked dog as she did it.

"Oh, come on Sheriff," Jonas said on behalf of the crestfallen lad, "We were never planning on getting into a sustained firefight here with anybody. Six rounds are plenty for a doorman."

"I know," she replied quickly, before catching herself and slowing down, "I know. I'm sorry, Colm. Altogether we've got

141

maybe thirty rounds or so for the revolvers, and twenty-five for the shotgun. It's thin, boys. Very thin."

Jonas stopped chewing his jerky and Colm hung his head. The sheriff grabbed a hunk of cheese and scarfed it down while she thought.

"Where's Leeroy?" she asked.

"Asleep in the back room. He had last watch. We slept in shifts. It was Old Bill's idea. I guess he remembers doing that during the war. At least that's how Leeroy tells it. You know Old Bill."

"Smart man, but it was damned foolish of him to run off like that. We could use him and his .45."

Jonas gulped down his jerky uncomfortably. Colm shifted in place looking at his boots. They were both wondering the same thing.

"Well, Sheriff. Pardon me for sounding ignorant, but… what *exactly* could we use him for? What is your plan?" Jonas asked.

"I can't pretend to know what they have planned for us, but you can bet it's something evil," Annabel said while trying to sound convincing. In truth, she wasn't so sure she truly understood the possessed men's motives, but she had a fair guess.

"These bandits aren't men," she said, "They're twisted reflections in the shape of men. To stop them, we'll have to kill them."

Colm turned the same pale white as Jonas' shirt, while the barman himself was looking at Annabel as if she'd said the devil himself had taken the town.

"Like that sick man you s-shot," Colm stuttered, "The marshal stuck his fingers in the guy's mouth and said something that scared Mr. Jeffries awful fiercely."

"That's right, Colm," she said, grateful that the kid seemed to accept it, even if he perhaps did not understand it.

"We tried to count how many of them there are out there, but no luck," Jonas muttered, "Leeroy said he thought about twenty."

"More or less?" Annabel asked.

"Not sure. He said it was difficult to keep track who were bandits and who were townsfolk. The way he tells it, they rounded everybody up and locked them in the stables."

"I'm going out there," the sheriff continued, pointing at the front door, "I'll need you to cover me from the windows with the other pistols you've got, but don't waste ammunition. Only take a shot with the pistol if it's clean. Use the shotgun to keep the outlaws from getting in. I'll try to make it to Duncan's to get as many weapons as I can carry. After that, if I can make it back here with them, we'll have a fighting chance. You take those torn up pieces of cloth and shove them into some whiskey bottles. If things get hairy light them up and throw them outside. I know these things dislike fire. It should keep them at bay if the bullets go before the killing is done."

Both men looked terrified at hearing the young woman speaking in such a cold and merciless way. Colm gulped audibly while Jonas nodded and made the bravest face he could.

"What about the man on the roof watching us?" Jonas asked, cautiously picking up the shotgun, looking uncertain and afraid.

"He's first."

Without another word, Annabel strode to the batwing doors and stepped outside.

Chapter XV

The street was silent and empty, the wind still and dead. Overhead the sun had just begun to ascend into the sky from the horizon, the early dawn light becoming stronger and brighter.

The sheriff took three paces from the saloon before the guard keeping watch on the place saw her. She saw the man moving, and smoothly drew the marshal's pistol and shot the cap of the man's skull clean off, the gunshot ringing loud and clear into the air.

She held and waited, the tip of her revolver still smoking. The waiting was hardest, but it was an important part of the thing. Keeping calm, taking careful aim, focusing the incredible rush of adrenaline that made her chest tight and her stomach cold.

A doorway opened from the general store to the left of the street. A man in a torn straw had stepped out, looking around with yellowed eyes slick with mucous and burning with hate.

These possessed men reminded Annabel of a rabid mountain lion she had seen once as a child. Much like the feral and diseased animal, these men became possessed with a frenzied madness at the scent of blood in the air. It was just like what she had seen in her office cell with Dweyer and O'Toole. But this time she knew what it meant and planned to use it to her advantage.

Walking with tall and heavy strides she approached the man, who was trying and failing to keep himself from frothing at the mouth with fury, almost as if he did not want the madness to overtake him. His hand was flailing awkwardly at his pocket, as if he did not have full motor control of the limb. Finally, he pulled a weapon from it, and he fumbled with what looked to be a small pepperbox pistol. Annabel shot him twice, blowing off his grasping fingers and tearing a massive hole in his diseased guts. He fell onto the general store's porch in a heap, oozing blood and black, tar-like bile.

The sheriff took a deep breath. Were these normal men with their faculties intact, they should be shooting at her right now. So why weren't they?

A gunshot rang out from the saloon, and Annabel spun around to see a crumpled body behind her. She could hear Jonas shouting from the saloon.

"Sheriff! Look out!"

She turned to face the main street and saw almost every door and shutter swing open, revealing faces tightly drawn with rictus grins of primal rage. She had expected it but confronted with the sight her knees shook in fear.

Wasting no time, she ran to the general store's porch while flipping open the loading gate of the marshal's revolver, working the ejector pin to expel the spent rounds.

She had barely managed to duck behind the cigar statue in front of the shop when the enemy fired the first bullet at her. The thing whizzed past like an angry hornet before burying itself into the lumber of the store's porch, causing an explosion of splinters.

Pulling two cartridges from her belt, she reloaded and peered carefully around the side of the wooden man she had hidden behind. Four in the street, in the open. Two or three on the barbershop porch. Another two near the bank. More coming from around the corner that led to the other side of town, she couldn't count. More than four, certainly, but less than ten.

Another shot from one of them sunk into the wooden cigar store statue with an incredibly loud crack. Annabel scooped up the pepperbox revolver from the man she had killed.

Bootheels clattered on the porch slats as the sheriff broke into a run, screaming across the street at a sprint and twisting at the hips to fire at the approaching mob. She winged one of the possessed before rolling into a crouch between two buildings on the other side of the street. The two men from the barbershop ran towards her, one of them bringing a lever-action to bear in her direction. Sickly gray pale hands held the weapon awkwardly, the tip of the barrel wavering about wildly as he fired.

A bullet tore through the air inches from the sheriff's eye before three more gunshots from her friends at the saloon connected with the gunman, sending him slumping into the street. The second one approached, while still wearing a barber's cape, his jaw dripping fresh shaving cream that had become mixed with blood and an oozing black ichor that dribbled from the man's open mouth. It took four slugs to put the screaming mutant down.

More gunshots continued from the saloon, and Annabel craned her neck around the corner to see the main mob from the street had been reduced to two slobbering madmen lumbering down the main street like mad, rabid apes. At the rate Colm, Leeroy, and Jonas were firing, they'd be out of shells soon. Far too soon. She

147

had lost count of how many times they had fired, but it had felt like the trio of men in the saloon were shooting from fear.

It would be a hell of a trek to get clear across town to Duncan's. She had no intention of trying it right now with so many men gunning for her in the open.

Instead she hurried along at a crouch to grab the rifle from the dead man nearby. As she grabbed the weapon she screamed in terror as the mutilated dying thing suddenly made a lunge for her with powerful grasping hands.

"Mine! It's mine!" the thing screamed and clawed, tearing Annabel's vest and reaching at her throat while keeping an iron grip on its rifle. She put two into its face with her pistol and heaved the rifle free with her left hand.

Another man rounded the corner of the alleyway from the main street, swinging an enormous hunting knife. Razor sharp steel hissed through the air and made a deep cut across the sheriff's arm before she was able to back away.

She holstered the marshal's pistol and hissed as blood streamed from her wound before working the lever-action of the rifle and shooting the knife-wielding maniac in the chest. The force of the impact threw him back into the street, and she worked the lever again, ejecting the spent brass onto the ground before plugging the man again as he lay prone.

Annabel quickly drew and reloaded the pistol with the rounds from her belt. Three left in the belt, a full six in the gun itself. She checked the rifle and was dismayed to find it only had a single cartridge left.

The wind carried with it the acrid scent and taste of gunpowder, acidic and slightly sweet. It was thick in the air, like the smell of countless clouds birthed forth from barrels of hot steel. Dust from the road mixed with the gunpower, throwing a haze throughout the street that trapped the sun in it.

Even if she managed to spend only a single bullet on each target, there were too many of them. She raised the rifle and took aim down the street at the approaching throng of creatures, before having to pull back into cover as gunfire erupted from the street, accompanied by growls and laughter.

"That's it, Madame Sheriff!" a voice called, sounding like the man named Slate from the night before, "Come on out where we can see you, and we'll all head back to the saloon, there's no need for all this killing. You're just robbing our host of flesh my dear. Wasteful, really. All you're doing is slowing things down. Why don't you set down your guns and get back to the saloon?"

The men roared as Annabel waited, her mind racing. Making it to Duncan's was her only choice, and she could not allow these men to make it to the saloon. They were focused on her, and she intended to keep it that way.

"Bold talk for some slimy monster's puppet!" she growled, looking around for somewhere to go.

"Perhaps we'll stop by for a drink while you mull it over!" he called, "As I recall the whiskey over there is pretty good. Or maybe I'm in the mood for something *red*. What do you recommend, Sheriff?"

Out of options, Annabel ran back across the street.

Thunder and smoke filled the streets to the brim with fiery metal death as she ran, firing back blindly with the last round in the rifle before dropping it in the street. These men, despite being infected with toxic traces of an ancient evil, were still outlaws.

149

They had no concept of firing as a unit to minimize the amount of smoke their weapons were belching out. After the first few shots, Annabel was convinced they likely couldn't see her at all behind the bluish gray cloud they had formed.

Thankfully, the wind was still enough today to give her a few extra seconds before the fog dissipated. Annabel dashed onto the porch of the general store and barreled through the doors at a sprint, tripping over a display of brooms before coming crashing onto the floor, sliding to a stop against a heavy barrel of meal.

Panting and sweating, she quickly crawled to the counter and slid behind it, peering over the cash register at the windows. So far, it looked like she hadn't been followed. Yet.

That was good. These men were still *afraid* of her. Despite Slate's rooster crowing, he and his lot of bandits were afraid to die and were acutely aware of how deadly the young sheriff could be. She had already killed a handful of men on her own, with little more to show for it than a shallow cut across her arm. She pulled a cleaning cloth from behind the counter to bind the wound before looking around for any weaponry.

The drawer where Lucille kept her pistol was empty, which made Annabel curse quietly. Her spirits soon lifted at the sight of an unopened box of cartridges laying atop the store's safe. Apparently little Lucille had kept her revolver behind the counter unloaded, which was no great surprise. The thought of the shopkeeper loading a gun, much less firing one, was ludicrous.

Annabel shuttled the brass from the box to her belt until it was full and pocketed the few spares that didn't fit. From outside, she heard another gunshot. She slunk to the back door.

Creaking open like a coffin lid, the door swung out slowly into the open. Moments later bullets exploded through the thing, heavy wads of led tore through the door.

One of the outlaws hurried closer to examine his kill and opened the destroyed door to see Annabel holding the broom she had used to push it open with. The outlaw's face bloomed with confusion and disbelief before she shot him square in the forehead.

Stooping to recover the man's pistol, Annabel reloaded it and holstered the spare weapon at her side. She jogged past the general store towards the doctor's office.

Through the gap between the buildings, she could see Slate. He walked slowly down the street, searching for the sheriff. Two men flanked him on either side, all of them armed with guns. None of them had seen her yet. She was at a rotten angle to try and shoot any of them, and any shooting would reveal her position. If she didn't take the shot, they may switch focus and go after the men in the saloon.

Without hesitation, she took careful aim and pulled the trigger.

A man spun on his heels and fell to the ground, spraying blood from a gaping hole in his neck. Annabel thumbed back the hammer and fired again, dropping the man she had hit earlier in the arm with a clean shot to the chest. Her thumb worked the steel hammer again.

Slate saw her after the first shot, and as she made the second and readied her third, he fired down the alleyway and the bullet hit the side of the doctor's office right beside Annabel's face.

Splinters of wood buried themselves in her face, neck, and arm. She inhaled to scream and swallowed gun smoke and more slivers, her own weapon going off and blasting the wall as well as she stumbled blindly backwards. Tears welled up in her eyes. Rubbing them only made it worse, and she hobbled away from the doctor's office in a blind panic, sneezing and coughing from breathing in the debris. She attempted to retreat to the general store only to trip over the body of man she shot while still inside.

As she tried to stand, she felt a steely grip clamp onto her hand and pistol, while another stopped her left hand from drawing the spare pistol in her holster.

"Please don't shoot!" hissed a voice in a whisper, "I want to help. I can guide you to my office, quickly now!"

The voice was familiar to her, but she could not place whose it was. Without any other options, she found herself being pulled along by the stranger's grip and heard him open a door before she was led into the cool interior of a building.

"Good shooting there, missy!" Slate screamed from outside, his harsh voice muffled through the closed door or the building Annabel was now inside, "Take your time licking your wounds in there! My men on the trail will have heard the gunfire, and by nightfall we'll overrun you and your yellow-bellied friends in the saloon there and rip you open under the moonlight!"

"These are a rather unpleasant bunch of savages, aren't they?" the voice of her mysterious ally quipped, as he rummaged around the room. Annabel still could not see him, and the room was merely a dark blur when she was able to force her eyes open.

The stranger returned to stand in front of her, and with that same iron grip he pulled her revolver from her hand and placed something cool and smooth into it instead. It felt metallic.

"Rinse your eyes with that and be gentle about it. You've got slivers in them."

Annabel did as she was told, and as she calmed down, she recognized the voice. It was the undertaker. She was in his office next to the doctor's.

The water was cool, and she cupped her hands in it and rinsed her eyes out. They both stung and burned, but after a few passes she got most of the splinters and flecks of wood out of them. Her left eye had gotten the worst of it, and she felt as if she still had a sizeable sliver still in it at the outside corner of her eye. Tears streamed freely from it and ran down her cheek.

"How did you evade them when they were rounding everyone up?" she asked the tall man in a suspicious and pained voice. He laughed quietly.

"I see your injuries have done little to smooth over your rough edges, Sheriff. A thank you would be appreciated."

"Thanks," she said, becoming distrustful of the man who was still holding the marshal's revolver she had been using.

"I hid in a coffin from them," the undertaker said dryly, "Does that satisfy your curiosity?"

From outside she heard another shot, and a cry from one of the bandits. One of the men in the saloon must have returned fire and gotten one of them. Three more shots followed, followed by the sounds of bodies hitting the ground.

"It's good enough for now. Give me back my gun."

"This belongs to the strange man from the east, doesn't it? The foreign lawman."

"Yes. It does. Now give it back," she growled, extending her hand for it. The undertaker did not move.

For a moment, it looked as if he had no intention of returning the gun to her at all, his expression had become dour and somewhat hateful. It was as if he had become a manifestation of winter itself, cold and cruel and devoid of life. The moment passed, and he handed the weapon back to Annabel.

"Stay hidden here," she said, uncomfortable at the display, "Hide back in your coffin or what have you and I'll collect you later. I don't have the bullets to spare for a second gun out there."

"As you wish, Sheriff," he said with a slight bow. He turned to face a tall coffin and stepped into it before turning to face the girl.

"Good luck out there."

Thin fingers closed the coffin lid, and Annabel heard a click from inside, as if it had been locked. The thought made no sense to her, and she dismissed the sound as something else. Who would bother making a coffin that locks from the *inside*?

Chapter XVI

Pulling a few of the larger slivers from her cheek and neck, she crept up to the funeral parlor window to peek outside.

Slate and his remaining associate were across the street, hiding in the bank and peering up through a window at the saloon. On the bank porch, two men lay dead. One slumped over the railing and another sprawled out on the ground. Three dead men laid in the street. Two Annabel had shot, and a third felled by someone in the saloon. By her count there should be around ten of them left.

The bigger group from down the street appeared to have taken a position near her office and the town's only hotel, both buildings providing them excellent cover, and a good view of the corner that led to the stables and to Duncan's shop.

The hotel would be problematic. Even if she managed to get Slate and his partner in the street, she couldn't hope to uproot those men from a position that fortified.

First things first. She had to deal with the remaining men in the street. Readying herself and reloading the marshal's revolver, Annabel saw a glint of sunlight on something on the hotel rooftop and ducked just in time to avoid catching a bullet in her teeth. The wad of lead shattered the funeral parlor window and showered her with bits of glass. She scampered out of the way and caught her breath.

It was over. She was pinned. Between the men atop the balconies and roof of the hotel, and the two inside the bank, she had nowhere to run. Even if she made it out the back door of the funeral parlor, she'd have to run across open ground to Duncan's, while in clear view of every outlaw atop the hotel.

She waited for some sort of demands from Slate, but after almost half an hour she came to the conclusion that the man was done talking with her. His position was a strong and comfortable one. Slate didn't need to even try to breach the saloon's defenses, all he had to do was wait until his reinforcements arrived from the pines. Even if they didn't show up, whether he was bluffing or not, the man could simply wait it out until Annabel fell asleep or tried to move from her position.

Annabel cursed, feeling desperate and furious. She shook and fumed like a boiling kettle, sitting in the dark parlor feeling absolutely hopeless. She picked at her slivers in frustration, before stopping herself, realized she was doing little more than scratching up her face even more. She'd need a pair of tweezers and some time to pull them out one by one.

She stopped fretting over her injuries and tried to form a strategy. If she could get a message to the saloon, they could fan out and take the bank first, then her office, then the hotel.

"Arrgh! That doesn't work!" she growled, kicking at a chair with her boot.

They didn't have any rifles for that kind of precision shooting, and she had no way to contact the saloon, *and* they would still need a safe position to fire from. The hotel was four stories high.

The only other point higher was the top of the old Boot Hill, which was clear across town to the northwest.

She sat and relaxed her body, trying to rest as much as she could while staying alert. She had little choice left but to try one last gambit.

Near sundown, she'd take both pistols in hand and make a break for Duncan's. Hopefully, she could throw enough lead at the men at the hotel with both guns to keep them hunkered down long enough so they couldn't return fire until she made it inside.

In her mind she tried to picture how far away it was. Thirty-five feet? Forty? An impossible distance to cross in the open with almost a dozen guns trained on her.

Her head hung low like a lead weight. Days ago, this would have sounded preposterous to her. To know that the valley would be under siege by strange men touched by strange biology, with her as the town's lone protector.

Hours crept by at a crawl. The streets went back to their odd silence, with no one firing a shot. Although she suspected that had more to do with dwindling ammunition from her allies at the saloon than anything else.

Shadows grew long and stretched east as the sun approached Boot Hill, readying itself to set. Tired, sore, and with a face full of splinters, Annabel slowly rose to stand on weary feet. The moment she moved, she heard the crack of a rifle.

She dropped to the floor on her elbows and knees, covering her head, but there was no impact from any bullet. The funeral parlor was untouched. She rose slowly and glanced at the hotel. A body was hanging over the balcony railing by the waist. Another shot rang out and Annabel saw a flash of red in the dying light of day as a man on the hotel roof was blown apart. She stared mystified at the sight. It looked as if the shots were coming from the gravestones of Boot Hill itself.

The men atop the hotel began firing all at once, creating a storm of sound as they fired towards the west without reason. As they unleashed their volley with the setting sun in their eyes, another man was hit, his flailing body thrown from the roof as he fell with a crash onto the rooftop of her office.

Annabel readied herself to run as she watched the sunset shoot the outlaws down.

With a pistol in each hand, she ran into the street, glancing at both the bank and the hotel as she ran. If Slate or his accomplice saw her, they made no effort to shoot. As for the men atop her office and the hotel, they seemed occupied with other matters, trying to find cover from whoever was shooting them down from the safety of Boot Hill.

Skidding to a stop on the dirt road, Annabel turned to try to spot who was up among the tombstones aiding her. As she did so, she found herself staring straight into the setting sun, bright and unforgiving. She squinted and dispensed with trying to get a bead on whoever was up there. The shooters chose their position well. Anyone wanting to return fire would have to do so with the sun in their eyes.

Annabel jogged past the bank, staying low as the shooting continued. She heard a door slam from somewhere near her office or the hotel. Another gunshot from the hill was followed by a macabre scream that altered in pitch as the screamer fell to the ground from atop the hotel.

With both pistols raised, the sheriff briskly strode towards her office. A dead man lay on the building's rooftop, while another had fallen to the ground. She shot the body on the ground in the head just to be sure before stepping over the corpse and approaching her office door.

Dry wood snapped from the hinges as Annabel kicked the door open, leveling her revolvers at the room. She sighed with relief, seeing it to be empty. She swiftly approached her desk and pulled open the creaking drawers, pulling out small printed boxes of cartridges and shoving them into her pockets. Retrieving the spare shotgun that rested alone in a tall glass faced cabinet, she hurried back outside.

Slinking under the horizon slowly, the sun retreated like an orange wraith behind the headstones of Boot Hill.

The ground near the hotel was flecked with blood, and spatters of scarlet dotted its clean white siding. She suspected every one of the plagued marauders had been killed, shot down from the cemetery before they had time to even properly react. Still tense, Annabel checked the street, and nearly shot Colm as he emerged from the saloon.

"Colm! Get back inside!"

From behind him, Annabel saw another man emerge from the old bar. Old Bill walked out limping, his right leg bound with a twisted white cloth and a long wooden splint.

"It's alright, Sheriff," Old Bill said in his seldom-used voice, tired and dry as an old bone yard, "They should all be cleared out, even that loudmouth in the bank over yonder. Colm's a decent shot if he has a bit of time to line the thing up."

Annabel's boots scratched loudly on the dry earth as she walked across the town's main street, now littered with bodies.

"You two were up on the hill?" she asked, pointing towards the graveyard. Old Bill shook his head and grinned with a toothless smile.

"No ma'am."

Jonas stumbled from the saloon looking as pale as a doily, clutching his shotgun with white-knuckled hands.

"If all of you are here, who did the shooting?"

"Reinforcements," Old Bill said, nodding towards Annabel.

Turning on her heel, the young sheriff was shocked to see the marshal and the thin old man who was her host on the prairie. The marshal's arm was in a makeshift sling, and he grinned beneath his great black mustache.

"Evening, Sheriff," he said with his sly and comically charming smile. Beside him, the older ex-marshal harrumphed in disapproval. Both men each had long guns slung over their shoulders, and the old thin man wore a shotgun on his hip.

Annabel's eyes returned to the marshal's, black and shining in the setting sun. She could not help but smile at the lawman, thankful beyond measure to see him alive again. Old Bill struck a match and lit a small cigarette before walking to the sheriff and handing it to her. Her fingers moved on their own like clockwork, taking the cigarette and bringing it to her lips.

"Leeroy, Colm, and myself will make sure everyone is alright. Judging by how well the hotel was defended, I'd reckon that's where they took everyone."

"No," Annabel said in a plume of smoke, "I'm the sheriff, I'll do it."

"Anna, you've got splinters in your face and your legs are shaking," Old Bill noted, "You get yourself into the saloon with these two gentlemen and get yourself a drink. I'll see if we can't get Mr. Jeffries to take a look at those slivers as soon as I find him. *Rest,*" the old veteran commanded. Annabel nodded, too tired to argue with a man that stubborn.

Jonas led her and the two marshals into the *Rye in the Sky* through the swinging doors, and a few moments later she was comfortable seated at a table across from the two lawmen. Jonas seemed to be calming down now, focused with his routine of preparing drinks, his troubles gone as he worked. Annabel sat quietly with her cigarette, staring at the men as if they were ghosts.

"I don't know what to say," she began awkwardly, "I mean, I don't know how to thank you."

"A glass of this magnificent whiskey is all the thanks I need madame Sheriff," the marshal said with a shining smile, gently saluting Jonas as he approached and set down three glasses of golden-copper whiskey. The thin old man with the hooked hand picked up his glass and sipped it slowly, savoring the strong and smooth flavor of it.

"See what you've been missing, Hook?" the marshal said, wearing a self-satisfied look. Hook glared knives at the marshal as he spoke.

"Just because I chose to live a solitary life doesn't mean I'm ignorant to what I gave up for it," he said gruffly, "The fact that you'd even mention it after what we've just been through rings tasteless and crass."

"Moments like this are what we just fought for, Hook," the marshal said with a sincere smile before downing his whiskey, "I fully intend to enjoy it."

"Pardon the interruption, but how did Old Bill reach you all the way out on the prairie in time for you to make it back here? It's a two-day ride from there to here," the sheriff asked, coming to her senses as the whiskey burned the fear out of her.

"We were already heading this way when he stopped us," the marshal said, "If it wasn't for him we would have ridden straight into town and into that shooting-gallery these monsters had set up atop the hotel."

"What happened?" Annabel said, wincing as she absentmindedly touched her face.

Neither man spoke right away, both looking at each other. After a pause, Jonas came and refilled the marshal's whiskey and set down a wooden bowl of peanuts before retreating back behind the bar. Hook sighed and leaned forwards with his elbows on the table and began the story as the marshal drank.

"I was wrong to tell you to ignore the thing in the mine," he said, starting slowly, "I know that now, and I'm not afraid to admit it. After a talk, the marshal and I decided to ride back to head into the mine and kill this thing."

Annabel wondered what the marshal must have said or done to convince Hook to change his mind, but decided it was best not to ask. The more thought she gave to the idea of how persuasive and manipulative the marshal could be, the more uncomfortable it made her. She had trouble being certain of the things he said, what was true and what wasn't. Right now, she knew it was unwise to dwell on the idea, however. Whatever the marshal had done, it was ultimately for the best. If the two had not chosen to return to the valley together, Annabel and the entire town's population would be a part of the monstrosity living beneath the mine. Hook lifted his glass to his lips to sip his whiskey, and the marshal picked up where the old man left off.

"On the trail, just outside of town near the woods we encountered more men, like those in the town here and in the mine. And we ran into something else. Something far worse."

Setting down his glass, the marshal leaned in and stared down at the last dregs of his drink.

"I nearly cashed it all in on a hill in the dark. Something came at us that might have been human once. It was more twisted than even that girl was in the mine. We were spent, nearly out of ammunition and out of time when Hook managed to get a shot off to vaporize the thing. By the time we'd done so, two men with rifles came upon us, only to be cut down by your friend, Bill. He gave us the score, and we rode back to town with him, and followed his advice to set up on Boot Hill. We slept in shifts until the shooting started. We got into position to give cover fire but couldn't see you in the street from the graveyard. Once the sun was behind us and conditions were right, we rained thunder onto the hotel."

"So now what?" Annabel asked, "The three of us go down into the mine and kill the beast? You said it couldn't be killed," she said, looking at Hook. The old man leaned back in his creaking chair and sighed.

"Maybe not. But the marshal and I have a plan for that. Even if we can't kill it, we can stop it from spreading. This frontier cannot be allowed to decay at the fringes as this cancer eats at it. We'll cut it out one way or another."

"What's the plan?" the sheriff questioned, sliding her glass aside and pulling a sliver from her cheek. She was tired, tired of feeling like this town was no longer her own. The sheriff was ready to take it all back from the plaguelike monster that had seeded its rotting roots into her community.

Hook stood slowly and stretched, glancing briefly at the marshal before finishing his whiskey.

"I'll leave you kids to talk about that," he said, "I am in sore need of some rest, seeing as it may be the last shuteye I get in this world. I'll be at the hotel if you need me. Goodnight marshal. Ma'am."

164

Tipping his hat, the old ex-marshal slid in his chair and left the saloon. Jonas approached again with two new glasses, and the marshal smiled and took them both.

"After a confrontation like the one we've just had today, barkeep, you look like a man in dire need of a good night's sleep too," he said in his peculiar way, sliding a short stack of folded bills across the table to the man, "I have private business with your sheriff that I'd prefer to discuss alone, if you can afford us the use of your saloon for a time."

Jonas looked at Annabel, waiting for her approval before he left. She waved him away and nodded.

"Get some sleep, Jonas. You fought well today."

"You too Sheriff. For what it's worth, I've never met a braver soul," Jonas said, overwhelmed with emotion.

"Goodnight Mr. Abernathy," Annabel patted his arm as she said goodbye, and the marshal saluted the man before watching the bartender make his way back home, locking up the bar behind him before he left.

Standing slowly, cradling his broken arm, the marshal walked to the bar and turned to face Annabel as he leaned against it.

"As a man rarely at a loss for words, I find myself struggling to find any now that I really need them," he said, looking at his boots. Annabel snuffed out her cigarette and crossed her arms.

"Whatever your plan is you can count on me, Marshal. We've come this far together, haven't we?"

To her surprise it looked like this reassurance didn't comfort the lawman at all. He sputtered and looked up at the wooden rafters and licked his lips, searching for words.

165

"That's the thing of it actually. We've been through a lot together. You've weathered storms that would challenge the convictions of even the most courageous person and come out on top. Grit and willpower and a great deal of luck have seen you through the mine and what happened here today in town. But luck doesn't last forever. Sooner or later, she becomes fickle and will leave you high and dry. Even the best poker players this side of the Illuminated River know when it's time to fold."

"What are you saying?"

"Sheriff..." he began, before swallowing hard and changing his tone, "Anna, over the last few days I have gotten to know you. I've had a chance to get to know this town and this place, and I've seen how much everyone here needs each other, and how they need *you*. I've been working with the marshals for a long time, and I have never, ever, seen a place quite like Ganndo Valley. You have something truly special here."

"I feel like you've said something like this to me before," Annabel said, still confused and now becoming rapidly suspicious of where the marshal was going with this strange outpouring of sentiment.

"Ah shoot, I know," he murmured, staring out the window, which had gone black now that the sun had fallen.

"Well then spit it out."

"You're not coming with us," he angrily said at last, looking torn to say it. Annabel looked at him with shock, not believing what she just heard.

"The hell I'm not!" she shouted as she got to her feet, "You put me through the ringer with all this nonsense about monsters

166

and things that whisper death in the dark, and then cut me out when you have a chance to put a stop to it?"

"I never should have involved you in the first place," the marshal ran his hand through his tar-colored hair, "That was my failing and I'll own up to that, but it stops right now. I can't put you at risk like that."

Annabel laughed coldly.

"You don't get to pull back the curtain and decide whether or not I stay onstage. This is *my* town, and like you said, it's a place worth protecting. I'm the sheriff in these parts, not you."

"That's my point!" the marshal kicked at a stool, and took a threatening step towards Annabel, "You're a part of this community! These people need you. You keep them safe, you look out for them. You aren't doing them any favors by going down into that mine with us, where we're probably going to die."

"I thought you had a plan," Annabel shook her head with furious sarcasm, "Is your plan just to go down there and fall over dead?"

"I can't guarantee that any of us are going to get out alive. If things get dodgy, we're going to blow the entrances and seal the thing shut. You know what it's like in that mine, Anna," the marshal was vivid now, his cheeks red with fire.

"I do!" Anna drew closer to him, getting in his face and gritting her teeth, "Which is why I'd have to be crazy not to help you. You've got two good arms between you and Hook, you need the help."

"The valley needs your help! Men like Hook and I are shadows. We haven't got names, or families, or people who will miss us when we're gone. There is no reason for you to risk your life going after the monster in that mine." he howled, taking another step.

"When I pinned this badge to my chest, I knew the risks. If it comes down to it, I'd give my life to protect this place, and that's exactly what I'm going to do. If you want to stop me, I'd like to see you try. I know this land better than either of you, what are you going to do? Try and lose me on the trail?"

This close to him, Anna could see the conflict in his face, hidden behind a mask of anger. Even over the smell of his cheap, generic cologne and the stuff he combed his mustache with she could smell the blood and dirt on him. The man was worn down and beaten, driven to his limits. His voice softened as he spoke again.

"I can't lose you."

The sheriff didn't say anything. A moment ago, she was ready for their argument to come to blows, and now with those four words the marshal had taken all the fight out of her. She looked at him with tired eyes flecked with splinters and for the first time saw not the marshal, but just the man. He looked back at her, seeming more real than he had ever been before.

Her fingers, singed and dry, touched the shoulder of his plain grey jacket. In spite of the pain, the marshal wrapped his arm around her waist, pulling Annabel closer to him, pinning his broken arm to his chest as he held her. He closed his eyes and leaned in closer.

Creaking loudly, the saloon doors swung open. Annabel's head snapped to face the doorway and she saw Mr. Jeffries standing there, clutching his black doctor's bag with a look of embarrassment on his face.

Reluctantly, the marshal let go of Annabel. She felt a wave of longing wash over her, wanting more than anything for him to hold her again. He cleared his throat, and his peculiar public demeanor returned to him as he smiled at her.

"If you're really meaning to come with us, we'll be riding out tomorrow after breakfast. I'll come by the saloon here for you before we set out."

Unable to think of how to reply to him, the sheriff merely nodded. Giving her one last look with his eyes of polished coal, the marshal winked and turned to face Mr. Jeffries.

"Take good care of her, Mr. Jeffries," he said, patting the elderly physician's shoulders as he walked out the batwing doors and into the silence of night.

Chapter XVII

Mr. Jeffries delicately shuttled his shining metal tweezers back and forth from Annabel's cheek and a small bowl on the bar that now held several splinters. Despite how old he was, his fingers were practiced and careful, and Annabel almost couldn't feel it as he plucked each one from her face. While he worked his face was still red with embarrassment. Sitting across the table from her beside a bright oil lamp, he had spent the last half an hour working to remove the slivers from her face, working mostly in bashful silence, save for a few apologies.

The worst of it was over, and he had carefully pulled most of the splinters from her eyes, tiny little things no thicker than a strand of hair. It was incredible to Annabel, but Mr. Jeffries seemed to take no pleasure in it, and looked miserable with regret.

"I truly am sorry Sheriff," he said for the fourth or fifth time, pausing to wipe a spot of blood from her cheek with a kerchief before continuing his work.

"It's fine, Mr. Jeffries," she said to him again, trying not to move her jaw too much.

"I don't believe it is fine," he grumbled, "I interrupted your moment."

170

The sheriff turned her head and winced as a sliver was pulled roughly from her temple by her movement. Old Mr. Jeffries stopped and gave her a stern look.

"Anna, *please* hold still. I am nearly finished."

"What do you mean you interrupted our 'moment'?" Annabel said.

The doctor sighed and set his instrument on the table with a quiet clinking sound. He took a drink from his small snifter of brandy and cleared his throat.

"Annabel, do you remember the last time we sat down for coffee?" Jeffries asked plainly, setting down the glass.

"I do," Annabel replied while trying her best not to touch her face where the doctor had pulled the slivers free.

"We talked at length about how people see you and I. How I'm 'the doctor,' and you're 'the sheriff.' That these roles define us, but they are not all there is to us as people. The marshal is the same way, but his role defines him far more strictly than ours do. For a man like that to put his identity aside and to be himself isn't easy, and moments where men like him do so are rare."

"What's your point?" Annabel asked.

"I just would rather have shown up a few minutes later, is all."

Annabel scratched at her scalp and exhaled sharply.

"Leo, please just say whatever it is you want to say."

Mr. Jeffries didn't say anything at first. He downed the rest of his brandy and looked at her with a paternal tenderness that was a mix of sorrow and joy.

"For all of your adult life we've talked on and off about how hard it is to do what you do. Not just as the sheriff, but as a woman. You're as strong as they come Anna, and I'm not saying you need some man to be happy, but I know how lonely it can be without someone with you. With nothing but that badge to define who you are."

"We've talked about this before," Annabel said. "We've talked it to death. I know I'm more than the badge and the gun."

Jeffries sighed and shifted in his seat, trying to grasp how to explain it.

"When I get too deep in brandy and wax philosophical about my life, I have no regrets save for one. I regret not spending more time as *myself*. I spent so much of my life being the doctor, playing my part. Women have come into my life and gone out of it, and there are days where I truly wonder if I could do it all again, would I do it alone? You're still young. You have your whole life ahead of you. You shouldn't have to live it alone."

Annabel started to form a reply but lost it before it solidified in her mind. It had never occurred to her that Jeffries had been unhappy, or lonely. Now that she thought about it, she understood. She had told him more than once how she felt that her role as sheriff made her undesirable. Too masculine, too rough, too stubborn and forceful. Any kind of man she met in town was either old, as most of them were, or too young and stupid for her liking. The marshal was like someone out of a dream almost. He was exactly the kind of storybook lawman that dime novels wrote about. But those stories weren't true, they weren't real. And despite the chance that his feelings for her might be truly genuine, Annabel had to wonder if they were actually sincere, or just another facet of the character he played in his role as the marshal. It gave her pause, and despite her own feelings of attraction to the man, she wondered if he actually cared for her at all. She wasn't even sure if her feelings on the matter were entirely clear. She had been so swept up in that brief moment, so overwhelmed by the events of the last few days, she couldn't be sure if what she felt was love at all. Perhaps she, like Mrs. Mattingly that first day he rode into town, had fallen under the marshal's spell. Mr. Jeffries looked at her as she thought in silence, patiently waiting for her to look to him again before he continued.

"Seeing you with the marshal gave me the impression that maybe you found someone that you can be yourself with. When this is over, whatever *this* is, maybe you two can make some kind of life together if you can break from these roles you've taken. And I stumbled right into it and broke that spell between you."

"I'm sort of glad you showed up when you did," Annabel said slowly. Hearing Jeffries say "broke the spell," rang true to what she had just been thinking. That's all the moment was. A bit of storybook romance. A cheap illusion that felt for a moment like real magic. Annabel smiled to herself and scoffed aloud.

"Oh?" the physician asked with puzzlement.

"I like the marshal just fine," she started awkwardly, trying to collect her thoughts, "He's handsome and kind and he's a devil with a pistol in his hand, but I don't know if he's the kind of man I could really be happy with."

"Is it because of that awful cologne he's so fond of?" Mr. Jeffries asked. Annabel snickered and shook her head.

"No, but it isn't doing him any favors," she grinned, "it's just that he's a *shadow*. He grins like a huckster and wears a demeanor that isn't his own. Like a magician, or an actor playing a part onstage. On the trail he talked about living loudly and enjoying life and about how much he loves people, but something about how he talks about that stuff is just off."

"You don't think he actually believes those things," the doctor asked. To his surprise Annabel shook her head.

"On the contrary," Annabel replied, "I think he believes those things very much. He truly *loves* people. But the marshal is a glorified drifter. He has no real anchors anywhere, no real connections with individual people. The other marshal, Hook, is just like him. Both of them view close personal relationships as some kind of liability. Not to mention at the rate the marshal is going he's living on borrowed time."

"Anna, are you certain you aren't just seeing that part of yourself in the man? I know it's hard for you to trust people, but there's something real there beneath the marshal's veneer. He's just as railroaded by his role as you or I, what you're seeing is him living that role. He's a prisoner of it."

"If he is, it's by his choice. He told me he loves doing what he does and has no intention of stopping. That suit and mustache is who he *is*."

"Do you think he really believes that about himself deep down? That he's little more than a figure from a picture book?" Jeffries asked. "You yourself have a certain way you speak and carry yourself when you wear your badge, he has his own way of wearing his. What I just saw wasn't a man playing a part. He seems to genuinely care about you," Mr. Jeffries attested, holding his snifter in both hands and smiling gently as his spectacles reflected the lamplight.

"How can you tell what's genuine about the man?" she asked, "He's the kind of man who is invited to the dance, is the life of the party, but then goes home alone. I don't know if he can really have a meaningful relationship with anybody. That moment we shared was completely superficial. He's an attractive man who thinks I am an attractive woman. We're both tired and beat to hell and are desperately longing for some human contact and comfort. It makes sense we'd try to find it in each other. If I'm going to even entertain having some kind of relationship with the marshal, I need to know who he *really* is under that suit. And I don't think there is anyone there."

"Anna, if you're unsure about the man's motives, you're just going to have to *ask* him about it and trust him to tell you the truth."

"How can I trust him to tell me the truth when he won't even tell me his name?" Annabel said, regretting mentioning it in the first place.

Mr. Jeffries said nothing else, quietly adjusting his spectacles. He coughed and set down his glass to pick up his tweezers again.

"We'd best finish this up so you can get some sleep, Sheriff."

Neither of them spoke again until the work was finished. Setting the last splinter into the bowl on the table, Mr. Jeffries collected his bag and left after giving Annabel a brief hug goodbye. She was left alone in the saloon.

Desperate to have something to do, the sheriff picked up the empty brandy snifter and took it behind the bar to wash it. Her tired hands worked over the glass with a clean rag as she looked out over the batwing doors at her town. She was certain, over at the hotel, everyone was feeling a mixture of relief and fear at what was happening, all without knowing the true horror of what was going on. In the street she could see Leeroy and Colm collecting the bodies of the dead to cart them up to Boot Hill, working alongside the undertaker who had provided sanctuary to her during the battle in the streets.

All thoughts about the marshal began to evaporate as Annabel set the glass down and left the saloon behind, walking down main street. Dark windows were broken, bullets were buried in siding and in painted shutters, but the town was still there. The people would persevere. Even with the streetlamps unlit, she could tell the damage would be undone in time, and the horror would be forgotten. Walking past the stables, Annabel wondered if this would be the last night she would see this place. If tomorrow they failed, that was it. Ganndo Valley would be consumed by a primordial evil, swallowed up and forgotten out on the frontier.

She wasn't going to let that happen. One way or another, the creature would not take her town. Stepping up onto the familiar porch of her office, she turned to look at the town one last time before retiring to her office.

It was dark inside. The cell where Dweyer and O'Toole had been kept was still clean and empty, and served as a grim reminder of what was at stake. In her mind she could see them, mad with rage and rotting apart, and knew that was the fate that awaited the valley should she fail. Sinking into her chair, Annabel placed her hat over her eyes and tried to sleep, desperate for one last good dream before having to face tomorrow's waking nightmare.

Chapter XVIII

Dawn came back to the valley wearing a veil of grey.

Mist and fog hung in the air like ghosts, and the morning was sharp and cold. Overcast skies swallowed up the sun, and the air was cold and unwelcoming.

As the sheriff awoke, stiffly rising from her chair, she felt an ominous sense of dread slither down her spine to settle in her guts. Outside the streetlamps were already lit, and Annabel could see groups of people walking towards the stables. Getting to her feet, still dressed from the night before, she grabbed a box full of cartridges from her desk drawer and walked outside into the brisk and misty air.

Around the stables it looked like the whole town had gathered here. Mr. and Mrs. Mattingly, Duncan, and Leeroy were grouped together near the barn doors beside the stablemaster. Colm and Jonas were talking with Ned Williamson and his wife holding cups of steaming coffee. Mr. Jeffries was there as well, looking over the contents of a large canvas duffel set out on an old sawhorse. Old Bill and Hook were talking beside Old Bill's horse, which had been saddled up and made ready to ride. Off to the side, beyond the crowd of the town's other inhabitants, Annabel spied the marshal having a hushed conversation with the undertaker.

Colm's eyes lit up as he saw the sheriff, and he waved in greeting. A hush came over everyone, and at once the entire town was staring at Annabel.

"What is this?" she asked, feeling small and uncomfortable, like a bug in a jar being peered at by children whose faces were too close.

Hook pushed his way through everyone to greet her.

"We told them that you're riding out with us to take care of the 'bandits,' holed up in the mine," the old man said, "People just came out to offer what they can to help. Almost got into fisticuffs with Old Bill when I told him he couldn't come with us. We need someone with some brains to stay behind in case we fail."

Annabel glanced nervously at the townspeople, who didn't seem to understand what it meant should she and her companions fail. Too many of them were smiling for her to believe they grasped the stakes of their endeavor.

"Do they know, I mean, do they *really* know what's going on?" she asked. Hook shook his head.

"No. Just the men from the saloon, and even them I'd think can't really grasp the weight of it. It's hard for a man to come to terms with the fact that this world hasn't always belonged to him. It's been passed on reluctantly from older, stranger hands that still cling onto its edges. I'd guess after time muddles the clarity of the events here, folks will just remember this as a time when outlaws laid siege to their town to rob it. People love excuses they can easily explain."

A low crowing sound echoed in the distance, and Annabel put her hands in her pockets. The marshal caught sight of her and smiled weakly before making his way over to her.

"The coffin-pusher over yonder claims he saved your life yesterday."

"That's right," Annabel replied. The marshal looked dour and Annabel caught him giving a quick look of apprehension to Hook before he shrugged and smiled his huckster's grin again.

"What?" she asked.

"Think nothing of it, sheriff. That fact likely saved his life just as much as he saved yours. Mr. Williamson's missing cattle had nothing to do with the thing in the mine. It's not like his kind to keep people alive."

"You mean undertakers?" Annabel queried, still taken aback by the marshal's open hostility towards the undertaker.

"If that's how you like it," he said cryptically before changing his tone, "Mr. Jeffries has taken care of my arm as best he can, set me up with a bona-fide sling and a bottle of tonic for the pain, such that it is. I won't be able to shoulder my rifle without something steady to rest it on, but my open top should serve me well enough if I can get it back from you."

"Only if you can actually shoot worth a damn," Hook growled as the sheriff returned the revolver to the marshal, "Are you sure you're up to this, boy?"

Checking the cylinder was loaded, the marshal worked the hammer back and forth gently, testing it while he curtly chuckled.

"Nothing certain in this world or any other, Hook. Somehow, I always make do," he holstered the pistol and winked at the old man, who snarled magnificently at the expression.

The three of them took a brief moment outside the old stable barn to collect the supplies the townsfolk had gathered for them. Ammunition from Duncan in small boxes filled their pockets and saddlebags, packed alongside tonics and bandages from Mr. Jeffries. Weapons loaded and horses saddled, the three riders set out into the morning grey to face death and destiny deep beneath the earth.

The first hours of the ride were tense and silent. Even the marshal, saddled upon his ebon steed, was quiet and still. Hook rode with the solemn composure of a gargoyle, and Annabel found herself feeling hopeless and cruel hearted. There had been so much killing in recent days, more bloodshed than she could imagine. What made her feel sick is that it didn't trouble her at all. She looked these monstrous men, possessed or infected or whatever they were, right in the eye and shot them down one by one. How many had she killed in town yesterday? A half-dozen or more. Her eyes found their way to the marshal, wondering again how he kept up his veneer of gentlemanly charm. Perhaps over time with the Marshals he would become more and more like his companion Hook. Cynical, jaded, and unwilling to let people in. She feared the same thing was happening to her. Whatever happened down in the mine today, Annabel knew things would never again be the same.

They took their lunch in the saddle, eating bits of jerky and biscuits packed by Mrs. Mattingly earlier that morning. The woods grew taller and darker the nearer they came, and the wind hissed through the trees with wicked sounds, carrying a chill upon each flitting zephyr that blew forth from the wood.

Near nightfall, it had become so cold the travelers could see their breath, white and stark against the background of a clouded and starless night. No coyotes made any sound in the distance, and they heard no birdcalls. After setting up their campfire, Hook swallowed an icy breath and spoke, breaking the hours' long moratorium on speech they had held.

"It knows we're coming," he said, looking into the fire while he set down a tin coffeepot directly on the coals, "The critters out here on the prairie know it too. They've all lit out farther west to keep away from it. We're going to have a hell of a time getting down to the heart of the thing."

Annabel pulled her saddlebags from *Blunderbuss* and pulled out a few more biscuits and a wedge of cheese for the trio to share, sitting beside Hook at the fire.

"How do we kill it?" she asked. Hook looked sullenly into the fire and prodded the coffeepot with his hook. When he finally voiced his plan, it seemed to Annabel he almost regretted having to speak it out loud.

"That sawed-off in my saddle is a special kind of arm, sheriff. Uses a special kind of shell, but I've only got one left. If we can get close enough to the heart, we can end it. But I doubt the creature is going to lie down and take it. Every poor soul under its command is liable to be down in the mine waiting to stop us. It'll throw everything it can our way. Everything from using its hosts to play at our emotions, use tricks to fool or waylay us. There's no humanity left in the mine down there, and we cannot afford to bring any down with us. Shoot to kill, everyone and everything. I'm going to trust you with the Helspitter, sheriff. You're the best shot of the three of us and you have two working hands. The marshal is still awfully beaten and wounded, and I'm too old to make the descent into the pit with it."

Annabel eyed the grip of the scattergun in the mule's saddle nearby. It seemed preposterous that such a common thing could be enough to destroy a spreading malaise of evil such as the beast in the mine.

"As a contingency, I'll be setting the dynamite we've brought at the mouth of the passages at the central chamber where we were brought before," the marshal said, "That spot seems to be connected to every in and out of the mine. If we can't kill it, we'll blow the tunnels and seal it in. If we have time, you and I will make a break for the surface while Hook stays behind and blows the fuses."

Annabel stared at the marshal coldly and gritted her teeth, setting her half-eaten biscuit onto her lap.

"You're going to leave Hook behind to blow himself up? We can tie the fuses longer and light them on the way out. Does Hook have any say in this plan?"

"It was my idea," Hook said while he lifted the coffeepot from the fire, "Someone needs to stay behind to make sure if it comes down to it. I'm old and my run is closer to the end than either of yours. The marshal and I talked it over. This also assumes we'll even have time to do so. If we're down too deep and are forced to retreat, we might not have time for any of us to get out. Push comes to shove, I'll blow the damn thing with all of us down there if it means keeping this thing from swallowing that town and spreading out east."

"Are you worried it will seal the tunnels itself to keep us out?"

"No," the marshal answered, "Whatever has emboldened it to start taking townsfolk instead of stragglers and drifters has made it desperate. I'm not certain it would compromise its ability to spread itself out by cutting off avenues to bring people to it. It has to infect them directly, remember? It's got its thralls *expanding* the passages with that mining equipment we saw down there earlier. I think I have an idea why it needs so many more people now."

Hook eyed the marshal with curious suspicion as he handed a piping hot cup of coffee to the man, then to Annabel. She raised the cup to her lips, and at that moment she realized what it was doing.

"It's trying to leave the mine."

Hook choked on his coffee and coughed.

"I told you already, *it can't leave the mine*," he said, still hacking and sputtering, "The creature is a mess of flesh and oil when you get down to it, a viscous liquid mass trapped in the cracks and crevices of the rock itself. It can't move on its own. When I saw it last, it was half entombed in stone and ore, choked with bodies of previous hosts."

"That's what the mining equipment is for," the marshal said, "To dig it out."

"Unless they dig out the whole block of stone it's trapped in, it'll dissipate and spill out from the rock," Hook spat, "All that would accomplish is moving it deeper down into the earth until it collects in more fissures in the mine. And there's no way the entire population of the town could fit down in the mine."

"The townsfolk aren't meant to dig it out, it has enough men for that. The townsfolk are going to move it," the marshal said.

"And I suppose they plan to lug this thing all the way across the prairie here, through Ganndo Valley, and over the country?" Hook growled with sarcasm.

"*Veins of wood and metal*," Annabel murmured, "That's what Rosanna said to me. I thought she was talking about the mine. But she's talking about the rail. The townsfolk were going to be used to speed up work on the rail line. Once the train has tracks that reach town, they can expand them all the way here, load the rock that contains the thing onboard, and ferry it across the country. Anywhere with a train station becomes a vector for it to spread."

Hook dropped his cup from his now shaking hand, spilling the coffee onto the fire with a hiss. His eyes shook in their sockets, and the man was seized by a fit of grief.

184

"This is all my fault…" he whispered, his face hidden beneath the brim of his hat as he hung his head.

"No, Hook," the marshal said, laying a hand on the old man's shoulder, "The only thing at fault is the creature in the mine. We're going to make it right. Together."

Annabel watched the marshal comforting Hook and knew that the young lawman's words could do little to soothe the old marshal's pain. Something else was hidden beneath the old man's sorrow, something deep and personal. Hunting this thing was his redemption, and until it was dealt with, guilt would ride old Hook into his grave.

Lost for words again, the riders finished their supper wreathed in silence of the night, before trying to sleep under the weight of the horror in their hearts.

Chapter XIX

Dawn did not come the next day.

The world was a widow wearing black, cloaked in a shroud of heavy thunderheads. Color seemed to have abandoned the prairie in the night, leaving behind thick velvet carpets of onyx and gray. Breaking camp was rapid and terse affair. All three travelers were anxious and touched by the first gentle caresses of adrenaline, ready for the coming terrors they would stand against. Saddled up, they lit out across the dark open plain with fire in their eyes.

The day passed by them in a flash and soon they reached the woods. As before, the creature the marshal rode hissed in protest as they drew near the woods. Annabel could not help herself and laughed more from nerves than anything else.

"Gopher holes and snake-pit again, huh?" she chuckled. At first the marshal looked gob-smacked by the comment before he nervously laughed himself, sighing with relief and feeling the tension ease slightly.

"Something like that, I reckon," he replied. Hook shook his head and smiled himself, which looked like it made him immensely uncomfortable.

They left their mounts untethered before entering the forest. The marshal and Annabel both un-hitched their heavy saddlebags, laden to the brim with sticks of dynamite. Annabel checked the fuses and threw the leather flap closed over the explosives after doing so, nodding grimly to the marshal. It was every charge left over from the old mining days, and they could only hope it was enough should things twist in a bad way once they delved into the mine.

More ominous and cruel than they had been before, the trees stood like strange alien limbs raised to the blackened sky, painting the vale with jagged patches of darkness. Needles and leaves crunched underfoot as the three walked across the forest floor with their weapons drawn. Sheriff Annabel and Hook carried lever-action rifles, while the marshal wielded his six-shooter. At his hip, the marshal carried another .44 given to him by Duncan, and both Hook and Annabel were armed in a similar fashion. Annabel bore two revolvers on belts that crisscrossed over her hips, studded with cartridges, and she carried a heavy shotgun over her left shoulder. Hook had his own revolver at his right hip, and the Helspitter set to cross-draw at his left. Armed and ready, the trio stalked the wood slowly, keeping watch for any of the possessed thralls lurking among the pines.

Drawing nearer to the pit where the marshal had fallen days before, Annabel signaled for the men to stop, and pointed forward in the dark. A thin plume of smoke rose from near the edge of the crevasse, from what might have been a small campfire.

"They were out here recently," she whispered, "But something made them leave their camp behind."

"When we saw the woods last, there were men posted at its borders with weapons too," Hook said, "There are no sentries out here at all. *Why*?"

"Maybe they're making a play for another attack on the town?" the marshal guessed.

"No," Annabel said quickly, "We would have seen them on the ride here. The prairie is too open."

In the distance to the north of the smoke the tear in the ground gaped open, appearing like a pool filled with primordial darkness. The marshal took a deep breath and pointed at the ground. Annabel strained to see what it was in the dark and caught sight of the rope she had used to reach him earlier.

One at a time they descended the heavy rope into the chasm, wearily eyeing the black for any signs of hostility. After Hook's heavy field boots thumped onto the ground, he led the way into the chasm. The passageway was narrow, yet Annabel thought it looked bigger than it had before. She guessed the presence in the mine had bidden its servants to continue digging all this time since she had escaped this place days ago. Fresh rock and galena were strewn about the ground, and after a short distance the welcome light of oil lamps illuminated the glistening rock in tones of orange and amber. Minecarts laden with rock and ruin were pushed to the side of the tunnels, and new rough support beams had been hastily constructed to prevent the mine from collapsing on the possessed workers. At least the trio would have cover if they were fired upon by the infected.

At last they had reached the large antechamber where Rosanna had been, Annabel felt something twist in her chest. Guilt bit at her insides as her companions spread out to examine the room. The only sign left that Rosanna had ever been here was a dark, oily stain near the center of the room. The marshal's eyes fell on her, and he paused his search while he approached her.

"You going to be alright, sheriff?" he asked gently. Annabel spit onto the rock and sneered.

"I'll be alright when that thing is dead and buried."

Hook whistled quietly in the dark and waved the two over to him with his hook glinting in the lamplight. He pointed to one of the tunnels that led from the antechamber that had been worked more heavily than the others. The passage was enormous, easily three times the size of the others in the cavern.

"I'm guessing this is the one that leads down to the thing," he whispered hoarsely, "You two set the dynamite, I'm not going to have the easiest time weaving those fuses together. We'll want the lion's share of it here by this passage, but we'll also need enough to seal off these other openings here. Anywhere a man with a pick can reach needs to be cutoff completely."

Shouldering his rifle, the marshal checked his saddlebags of dynamite and sucked his teeth.

"These tunnels are bigger than they were before, and not just this main passage either. All of them have been worked. I'd agree with your reckoning that this mammoth one here leads to the creature below, but to be sure we'd have to blow every single one of these. I'm no demolitionist, but I'd guess we'd need maybe twice the dynamite we've got for a job like that."

Annabel and Hook stared at the marshal for a moment in disbelief and horror.

"Marshal, we've got over two dozen sticks with us here, easily. There are only five passages. Shouldn't that be enough?" the sheriff asked.

"There's no way to know unless we actually try to blow them all. This dynamite is old, sheriff. While that makes it more dangerous, it also makes it more uncertain if they're still potent. Dynamite sweats out the nitro in them over time. Unless these

189

sticks are lined with wax, or their box has been turned over every once in a while to keep the sorbent from separating from the nitro, some of these may be incredibly weak. Some might not blow at all or blow early if they're hit hard enough by something."

"How the hell can you know that? You *just said* you weren't a demolitionist," Annabel hissed, louder than she meant to. Hook sighed and hung his head.

"I'm a marshal, Anna. I know a little bit about everything. When I puzzled out this plan, and when I realized the thing down here needed the townsfolk to work the rail line, I hadn't considered it would have started digging already. What we brought would have been enough if these were the same diameter they were when we last had our little visit down here."

"So that's it. Our gambit now is to kill it with our one shell we've got in the Helspitter," Annabel growled in defeat. The marshal shrugged.

"We've got two options," the marshal said, "We can set what we have at each of these tunnels, and if things go sour down there, we hope it's enough to blow the tunnels. Or we set everything in the main tunnel that leads to the surface and knit the fuses together so we can reach them from here."

"Marshal, if we do that and have to blow it, we'll all be trapped for certain," Hook interjected gruffly, "You prepared to give up a shot at you and Annabel getting out of this alive?"

"I'm prepared to do whatever it takes to stop this thing," he replied, his black eyes gleaming. Annabel cleared her throat.

"Let's do it," she said, "We pile all of it at the junction near the pit. If we go down it goes down with us."

190

"Good lord, she sounds like one of us, doesn't she?" the marshal said with a wild grin as he and the sheriff began making their way back to the passage to the surface, "For what it's worth, you'd make a damn fine marshal yourself, Annabel."

"I don't know if I should feel proud or insulted," she said as she walked alongside the man in grey. Once they reached the entrance they began slowly and carefully setting the saddlebags filled with the dynamite onto the rocks near two of the support beams, twisting the fuses together to make one long twisting cable they could lead back to the antechamber.

After the charges were set, the two returned to Hook and began their final descent into the abyss.

Chapter XX

Rock crumbled and rasped beneath their boots as the two marshals and the sheriff made their way into the unknown depths of the mine. As they went deeper, light from the flickering oil lamps caught on bright veins of unworked silver that glittered coldly in the shadows. A veritable fortune had been buried down here all this time Annabel had lived above, ignorant of the riches hidden so near Ganndo Valley. If it weren't for the creature that made this place its den, their town would likely have boomed and grown in an incredible fashion with rich deposits of silver like this so near. She watched the marshal's eyes light up at the sight, his mouth agape beneath his onyx mustache.

"There must be a few dozen tons of silver woven throughout this place," he said in a hushed voice, "I know you sold the townsfolks tales about the mine being worthless, but I can't believe no one ever bothered to check."

"Maybe they did," Hook replied somberly, "And look what became of them."

The marshal did not speak again.

Ahead the passage twisted, and the ground became uneven and slick with humidity, curving like a glinting serpent deeper and deeper into the world. Hook slipped on a patch of wet ground, sliding downwards with a curse until he stopped at the lip of the tunnel that dropped off into an enormous mine shaft.

A column of rock nearly a hundred yards in diameter had been cleared out and filled with a network of wooden ramps, stairs, and walkways. Platforms connected to pulleys by rope ferried rock and refuse up and down the deep cavern. Walking among the mine, Annabel could see scores of men and women toiling endlessly in the depths. Lamplight caught on faces drawn thin and blank, their eyes wept tears of thick viscous black oil and slime as they shuttled carts of rock along tracks on the walkways. Men whose forms had been mutated and twisted into mockeries of flesh and bone lifted picks in heavy misshaped hands, striking walls of stone with unnatural percussion. A few of them looked so old Annabel was shocked to see they were still standing, while others were so young it sickened her to her core.

White bones slick with filth and grime carpeted the floor of the shaft, which was nearly sixty feet deep. Some of them looked so alien to the sheriff she wondered if they were even human. Tools arrayed throughout the chasm told a strange story on their own, some fairly new, and others foreign and very, very old. The marshal cocked his revolver and gritted his teeth.

"There's one tunnel down there at the bottom of the shaft," he whispered, "That has to be it. Was it like this when you were here last, Hook?"

"No," the old man answered, "This is *worse*. This is where he fell, there was no sound back then. Just a great yawing darkness. Yet now… all of this is so much worse."

Carefully lowering himself down onto a platform near the tunnel they were standing in, the marshal crouched down and scanned the possessed working the mine. A few of the men he had seen camped outside guarding the woods were here. Infected outlaws and bandits who carried guns. Hook eased himself onto the creaking planks of the platform and began gently nodding slightly as he counted them. Annabel followed the two men onto the walkway and shouldered her rifle. Before she had a chance to get a count of how many of the possessed carried firearms, every single body in the shaft stopped moving all at once.

With a slow synchronized movement, they all turned to look up at the three intruders that were crouched atop the chasm. Annabel felt her heart in her throat, and the marshal's face paled a shade of grey that nearly matched his shirt. Hook's brows furrowed and his eyes narrowed. From somewhere unseen a voice called out, low and so inhuman it made Annabel's teeth hurt.

"What bait willingly hangs itself on a Hook like yourself, old friend?"

To Annabel's surprise, Hook stood from his crouched position, tall and proud in the dim orange light.

"This has gone far enough!" Hook shouted into the abyss while nearly a hundred watchful pustulant eyes gazed at him from the dark, "This has to stop, Deacon!"

"Deacon?" the marshal whispered, gazing up at Hook's face, tight and strained with grief and anger.

"You speak no comfort to me, Hook. Have you forgotten what I lost so that you might live? Now you come here with a fledgling marshal drowning blindly in his own broken ideology, and the local law driven by grief and rage. Leave them here and return to the prairie, Hook. Leave them to become a part of me. You have never stopped me before."

194

"You were only taking evil men before!" Hook yelled, "Murderers and outlaws! I thought you needed them to survive, but you've just *enslaved* them. How could you do this?"

Beneath the walkways and platforms, the people within the chasm began moving again, taking up tools and weapons into their hands. The few who carried guns began positioning themselves slowly near the edges of the platforms upon which they stood. Annabel shifted her view from threat to threat, watching them closely from behind the sights of her rifle. The marshal kept his revolver raised in his hand, pointed at Hook himself. The old man caught sight of it and looked at the marshal with resigned sorrow on his face.

"You *knew*," the marshal said through gritted teeth, "That's why you stayed on here on the prairie. You lied to me about why you hesitated to kill it before. It wasn't some kid in the mine. It's because the thing melded with Deacon, isn't it? You knew it was still down here and you knew it was taking people. *Why?*"

"Why?" the creature repeated in resonant, mocking tones.

"Deacon was my friend," Hook said quietly as Annabel watched the marshal, his revolver pointed directly at the old man, "We had killed its thralls and tracked it down to this place and found the creature bonded to a local outlaw named Harrigan. He had gone mad, and the thing had warped his already twisted mind enough to drive him insane with bloodlust. It drew me towards it… Did something to my mind. Before it pulled me into its embrace, Deacon threw himself between us and it took him instead. It melded with him…*infected* him. He gave me his Helspitter and begged me kill him and I couldn't. It was still Deacon. I still loved him."

195

"So you helped him become a monster?!" the marshal shouted. Annabel heard two score voices laughing below and felt the rumbling terror of the creature itself laughing with them.

"I am no monster. I fed upon the cruel, the wicked, and the profane. Our arrangement was noble, and our cause was a righteous one. Ganndo Valley has prospered and flourished under my care."

Annabel bolted upright herself, standing over the creature's thralls with her weapon ready in her white-knuckled hands.

"You preyed upon my town and my people!"

"Dear Sheriff Annabel," the creature cooed and growled hungrily, **"I preyed upon no one your little settlement would miss. O'Toole and Dweyer were thieves and liars that plagued the valley for years, and I unmade them. Every man you shot down in town days ago was the same or worse. Drifters and criminals who came to prey upon your people, to slake their unnatural appetites for blood and flesh upon your innocent townsfolk. I am your unseen champion, Sheriff."**

"What about Rosanna?" Annabel said with hot and angry tears in her eyes.

"She came to me on her own. I needed her. She helped to guide others to me willingly. I learned things from her, here in the dark, about the world and how it has changed since I have been kept here. She taught me the most important thing of all. *All men are wicked.* Not one among your blighted race can be trusted to do good for its own sake. You seek to stop me and save your people for personal, small reasons. Revenge. Guilt. Duty. But what are you really saving them from? Becoming part of something *better.* Something *more.*"

196

"How is this better?" Annabel asked, gesturing to the mindless thralls below.

"Humanity has been divided since the dawn of time. I seek to unite them in a way that has never before been conceived. Something out there in the dark is waking up, and the world of men cannot be trusted to face it divided as they are. I can *save* them from themselves. Once we are all connected by this being that has become a part of me, we shall be as one. Free from bigotry, free from doubt, free from pain. No nations, no races, no wars. One people. One nation, *indivisible.*"

"Deacon, please," Hook pleaded, lowering his rifle, "You cannot truly believe that. This thing is clouding your mind, it's polluting your thoughts. You have to *fight it*. You know this is wrong. We have to finish what we started all those years ago. I couldn't save you then, so let me save you now."

Silence followed. The walking possessed held their ground for a brief moment, still watching the three people high above them on the platform near the exit passage. A growling sound emanated from the pit below, echoing throughout the primeval cavern.

"If you cannot see the light of reason, then you will be drowned in the dark."

"Deacon, don't!" Hook cried.

At once the creatures in the dark screamed and wailed like rabid banshees and began clambering across the platforms and walkways with death in their bleeding eyes.

A tide of bodies rushed the sheriff and her companions on the walkway with madness coming off of their feverish bodies in waves of profaned heat.

Annabel had begun shooting almost immediately after the creatures screamed and began their charge, focusing fire on the few infected men that held their own firearms, who had unleashed peals of gunpowder-born thunder themselves as they fired upon her, Hook, and the marshal.

Darting down the walkway like an ashen ghost, the marshal fired his revolver into the throng of rushing mutants, lining up each shot for a quick and lethal end to the nightmare creatures before being forced into cover under a hail of lead. Hook worked the lever action of his own weapon with his steely appendage, pulling metal on metal as he chambered additional rounds after every crashing shot.

Annabel pushed forwards to descend a wooden ramp to reach cover with the marshal behind a few minecarts as wood splintered and exploded around them. Bootheels clacked madly on the timbers as they ran, snapping off shots as best they could as they descended.

Shots rang out overhead and ricocheted off of the stone walls of the mine and the metal bandings on the minecart. The marshal hurriedly and clumsily reloaded his revolver with his injured hand while Annabel and Hook also reloaded their own guns.

"We have to get down there!" Hook yelled over the gunfire, "The longer we stay up here the easier it'll be for them to pin us down."

The old man drew the Helspitter from its holster and held it out to Annabel.

"Take it and finish this! I'll cover you from here," Hook pulled a book of matches from his vest and handed them to the marshal.

"You need to get back up in that chasm and light the fuses."

"That won't give us very long!" he yelled, ducking as a bullet sliced through the air above the cart.

"Those fuses should give us ten minutes! If it's not all over by then these things will get us long before that! Go!"

Hook stood and fired rapidly into the dark, working the lever with mechanical precision as he cut down four of the grabbling monstrosities as they drew nearer up the walkway. The marshal made a rolling dive to the side and bolted up the passage where they had entered while Annabel holstered the Helspitter and ran down a gangplank, firing as she went.

Scrambling up over the uneven stone edge of the passage, the marshal ran full tilt beyond the passage and was forced to dive to the ground as a bullet raced past him, tearing into a support with a crack. Hurrying to his feet and ignoring the blood blooming at the elbow of his jacket, the man powered forwards across the rock with sweat dripping from his nose. Reaching the edge of the tunnel, he found the fuses twisted together like strands of twine and knelt on the damp stone to light it. Hook was right, they wouldn't have long before the charges went, maybe ten minutes to find this thing and end it. At the core of his being, the marshal felt betrayed knowing that the old ex-member of his fraternity had consorted with this thing to keep his friend alive. Putting himself in the old man's position, would he have done anything different had Annabel been taken by this horror?

Shuddering to think of it, the marshal wiped the perspiration from his brow and struck a match against the book and lit the entire thing, setting it down beside the fuse. Springing to life with sparking ferocity, the fuse sputtered and hissed as the flame began to slowly snake its way through the mine towards the payload of dynamite.

"It's in your hands now, Sheriff," he muttered to himself, reloading his revolver and beginning to race back to join Hook as the old man covered Annabel's descent.

Chaos and death danced a frenetic twisting waltz in the chamber.

Hook stood atop the platform near the exit from the passage, raining death upon the mutated possessed as they tried to reach him. He had ceded ground under their assault, moving back towards the mine carts after trying twice to gain ground. Blood ran freely from walkways and gangplanks, tainted with black bile and chips of bone. His hook worked the lever of his rifle until the firing block refused to move again. He dropped the rifle to the ground and drew his pistol, thumbing back the hammer he put two rounds into a burly woman approaching a ramp that led to Annabel.

Below him, Annabel ran as fast as her legs could carry her, darting across shifting and weak walkways rotted away by time. Her rifle had given out before she had made it down the first two landings, and she now kept the mutated masses at bay with a revolver in each hand. A bullet bit into her hip and she cried out in pain before training her guns on her attacker and firing both barrels into him, sending the possessed rifleman flying into open air and plunging to the cavern floor.

Limping now, she rushed forward with an ungainly stride, driving nearer towards the next ramp downwards. She was close to the pit now, maybe twenty feet above it. Overhead she heard Hook shout something and couldn't turn to look. Two manic creatures far more twisted and distorted than the rest came shambling towards her, their bodies torn open in horrific unnatural ways. Annabel pulled the triggers of her revolvers, and only the gun in her left hand responded, the other weapon empty. She threw the empty revolver at the one creature she hadn't shot in an attempt to slow it, but to no avail. The thing barreled into her and sent her flying off of the walkway, and the two of them landed with a thud on the edge of a platform below. Annabel screamed with pain and fury as the thing atop her tried to rend her apart with its bone-like fingertips raking across her shoulders and back.

Rolling over, she pressed the barrel of her revolver underneath it's chin and pulled the trigger, showering both of them in gore. The thing shuddered in its death throes as Annabel strained to push it off of her, pulling herself into a kneeling position. She pulled cartridges from her belt to reload her gun, dropping several from her blood covered hands. Another creature had begun to approach her before its head exploded suddenly as the marshal shot it from atop the cavern.

Her weapon reloaded, Annabel got up and continued to hustle with her injured leg into the enormous yawing tunnel before her, blinking blood and tears from her eyes. She tasted earthen grit and copper on her tongue, and her hip was on fire. None of that seemed to matter now, she was close to the thing. She could feel it, feel the bass of its heartbeat in her chest and between her ears. The passage was lit with candles set directly onto the rocks, and as she pressed onwards the sounds of carnage and gunfire from the adjoining chamber became muffled before fading almost to silence.

As she walked the mine's tunnel, a buzzing thrumming sound began to build in her mind. The sound was like a hive of hornets in her head, and she felt them shaking in her jaw. Her vision blurred and became weaker, almost like something was taking a hold of her. Shaking her head violently, she drowned it out and soldiered forward.

Ahead the light was brighter still, and she could see the off-white tallow of perhaps one hundred candles arrayed upon the centuries-old stones. The passage ended abruptly at a small chamber, no bigger than her own office back in town, that reeked of must and stale flesh mingled with old ghosts. In the flickering candlelight, she could see something glinting at the edge of the room. Something slick and wet, that shone like oil reflecting ribbons of rainbow colors in the sun.

The stone itself was a great slab of smooth rock unmarred by ore. Tendrils of slick primordial tar leeched out from the rock, running down cracks in its surface until they came into contact with a nearly mummified human body melded with the bones of at least three other skeletons.

Black cavernous eye sockets stared blindly out from its skull, its lower jaw broken down the center between the teeth, gaping wildly open. Veins of alien material snaked between its ribs like webbing, that looked like mycelium to Annabel. Rusted buttons from a jacket long since rotted away had fused to its chest, and a time-eaten leather belt of faded black encircled its skeletal hips. In the holster it wore was an old Dragoon that looked much like the gun the marshal wore. Most telling of all was the badge woven to its chest by threads of living material, a small silver star set into a ring that bore strange runes upon it. Annabel found herself in awe of the thing and forgot herself as she examined it. She stowed her revolver at her hip and drew the Helspitter. Without moving, the corpse before her sucked a breath of stale air and spoke to her, much more quietly and weakly than before.

"Please...don't," it hissed feebly in a voice that sounded like a gentle breeze rustling dead leaves.

"The others you have slain were a part of me. A willing part... My only wish was to unite us all. No war... No sorrow... Only peace..."

Annabel found her finger on the trigger, but she was unable to squeeze.

"You're a blight on peace," she said gritting her teeth, willing herself to shoot. Her finger couldn't move. That buzzing sound in her head had fallen into her limbs, which ached and felt half asleep with pins and needles. Her hand shook just to hold the Helspitter.

"I swore to preserve life, and I have preserved it," the thing said, "It has bloomed at my touch. I sacrificed my humanity for it... Those souls in the mine outside, the ones being cut down by those killers in grey, they are alive in a way they could only dream of."

"What you've done to them is worse than killing them," Annabel strained to say, wondering how much time she had left before the dynamite went, unable to move even to keep the sweat from her forehead from dripping into her eyes.

"So you say. Yet it was you, not I, that killed that girl, Rosanna. My sweet Rosanna... my prophet..."

Annabel hissed and shook in place, feeling blood run from her left nostril as she fought against the alien thing's mind.

"I know you're still in there somewhere, Deacon," she grunted as her jaw clenched shut, "This thing has a will of its own, it's polluting your thoughts and twisting them. Look at what you've done, what you've stolen from these people. Remember who you are! Remember what you stand for!"

"I have done more for what I stand for now than I could have ever thought possible as a lone, frightened human. The Stranger does not forget."

Annabel felt her right foot lift from the ground and step closer towards the thing. Fighting with everything she had, she shouted and tried to force herself from approaching the creature. Thick slime oozed from the cracks in the stone, reaching out towards her.

"It will be over quickly, Annabel. Soon the comfort of unity will wash over you, and you shall be at peace. One among many. Needed. Wanted. Loved."

Losing the fight with the dark locomotion driving her forwards, Annabel took another step towards the creature's putrescent grasp.

Chapter XXI

Throwing his pistol aside, Hook drew his knife in his open hand and raised his hooked hand as he took a defensive stance atop the walkway. Beside him kneeling on the old wooden platform, the marshal wiped blood from a cut over his eye he had suffered while diving behind a minecart. Out of cartridges and nearly out of time, the two men knew they were nearly finished.

Drawing his own knife, the marshal dropped it onto the platform from his trembling fingers that were nearly numb from pain. Hook knelt and placed the weapon into the young marshal's hand as he looked into his eyes.

"You plan on dying without a weapon in your hand?" he asked, attempting to smile. The marshal laughed and pushed himself upright with his elbow, wincing in pain.

"I try not to plan on dying at all if I can help it," the marshal said, still gripping the handle of the blade to the best of his ability, "Never thought I'd buy it getting blown to kingdom come by dynamite I set myself though."

"Life's funny that way," Hook said, watching half a dozen mutated monstrosities clambering up towards them, bounding over countless corpses of the other abominations the two lawmen had shot down.

"I wish I'd told Anna I loved her," he said, his mustache falling as he realized this was the end.

"I wish I had told Deacon I loved him more often," Hook muttered, clutching his knife and snarling beneath his beard. The creatures continued racing closer and closer, torn apart and laden with claws and fangs that bloomed from exposed red flesh.

One of the beasts had rushed ahead of the others and made it beyond the edge of the platform where the two men held out, leaping towards Hook with a howling scream. The old man slid forwards and sunk his knife into the creature while leveraging his hook to throw it over the walkway into the darkness below.

"Come on then you wretched mongrels!" he shouted, "Come try your hand with the marshals!"

The creatures drew nearer as a tide of blood and death.

Limbs moved on their own, pushed forwards by an arcane and ancient will outside of her own, as Annabel took yet another step towards the creature. Its form had bloomed from the rock and the corpses of Deacon and countless others like him, a mass of tentacled oil and bile. It reeked of sweet death and mold, and Annabel retched as she continued to fight against the mental commands of the thing before her. The tangle of corpses and black bile shuddered and twisted in place against the rock as she took each reluctant step, dribbling filth onto the dirt beneath it.

Frantic and still gripping the Helspitter, Annabel forced her lips apart and brought life back to her rigid tongue in an attempt to speak. She was maybe three feet away from the creature now, and if she could not fire the weapon in her hand, all was doomed.

Sensing her attempt to defy it, the creature rumbled with cruel laughter that sounded to Annabel like all the hells had opened up before her.

"Defiant to the last. What remaining mindless pleas could you possibly voice so close to your embrace? Humankind is a murderous avaricious blight on this world. What could you say to defend or preserve such wicked, irredeemable creatures who cannot be trusted to save themselves from the coming horror?"

"W-we are the nameless..." Annabel croaked. The thing before her became a flailing engine of wrath at the words, inarticulate in its rage, yet she had stopped walking. Forcing her jaw to move, she continued.

"The riders in the night..."

Out in the main chamber of the cavern, the thralls that remained before Hook and the marshal ceased their approach, and began convulsing in place, a mess of chattering teeth and

207

crunching bone. Hook watched them wearily with his bloody knife in his hand, while the marshal forced himself to his feet.

Deep in the pit before Annabel, the creature's heart began growling and howling, and the sheriff could hear a multitude of independent voices slowly beginning to emerge as it cried out. Her muscles began to feel more alive, and she pressed on with the oath

"We are the faceless, who raise the shining light."

"Stop! Still your chattering tongues! We are one! We are a perfect union!"

"We are the fearless, and never shall we fall," she continued, stepping closer now, emboldened by what she knew was right.

"Enough!"

"We are the marshals, that keep watch over all."

Writhing and twisting with increasing violence, the creature's madness robbed it of all reason. Limbs tore themselves from the mass of viscous black liquid, falling to the floor in heaps of bleached bone and mummified flesh. The oldest bodies began to fall away, and as they did the voices became less and less numerous, as the creature's hold weakened on them. Deacon had found himself within the beast, and was fighting back, remembering who he was and what he stood for. A single voice called out to Annabel from the creature drowning out all others in bright and clear cadence.

"Shoot Annabel! Kill it now!"

Annabel squeezed the trigger.

Sapphire flames exploded outwards from the barrel and tore the creature apart in swaths of fire, vaporizing the beast. The recoil threw Annabel's body stumbling backwards as she struggled to stay on her feet, still weak from resisting the monster's mental control. The voices were silent now, and the cavern grew dark again as her eyes struggled to adjust after being blinded by the burst of light from the Helspitter. She turned to leave before stopping herself, quickly approaching Deacon's remains to retrieve his badge from the ashes of his bones.

Annabel began sprinting as fast as she could, ignoring the agony in her hip where she had been shot. It seemed to her that she was far too late already to make it out of the mine before the dynamite blew, but she had to try for it. Her boots scraped along dirt and rock as she ran full tilt, clutching Deacon's badge in her hand. She emerged from the passage at the bottom of the pit moments later to see the slumped bodies of a score of mutated hosts of the creature. Those that had not been killed by her or the marshals had fallen dead from injuries no mortal body could sustain, their twisted forms lay in puddles of blood and ichor on the ground. Looking up, she could see Hook waving to her.

"I'm coming up, you two head for the exit!" she shouted hoarsely.

"You'll never make it running all the way back up here!" he called back, "Stand on that platform there, the one with the ropes and pulleys on it. Hurry!"

Annabel raced to the platform, suspended from heavy ropes from a support arm above. Hook aimed with a rifle taken from one of the infected and shot the rope on the pulley cleanly in two, releasing the counterweight and sending the platform racing to the top of the chasm.

Rattling violently to a stop, Annabel nearly fell back down into the pit before the marshal weakly helped her up. His face was covered in dried blood that had matted his oil black hair.

"Come on sheriff we've got to go," he said, pulling her with all his might. Together they ran through the dark passage, stumbling and tripping over rock and debris, all the while the scent of the burning gunpowder fuse grew stronger and stronger.

Up ahead the marshal could see it, flickering and sparking drawing nearer and nearer to the passage. He pushed himself to the limit, his legs on fire and alive with biting exhaustion. Hook watched the light reach the end of the wicks near the dynamite and felt his heart sink into his stomach.

The marshal turned to look at Annabel one last time as he watched the reflection of the sparking fuse touch the dynamite in her eyes.

The passage exploded.

Chapter XXII

Earth and rock swam in the air like marine snow, particles of the dead intermixed with inorganic flotsam. The oil lamps in the passage had been blown out in the explosion, shrouding the ruin in darkness.

Shadows swam with clouds of dust and death in the mine, far from the nurturing light of the sun. The creature below had been destroyed, and with it all traces of its presence, collapsed in heaps of bone and blood in the chamber beneath them.

Among the ashes, something coughed.

Rising from a sea of grit, Annabel brought herself to her feet, still partly deafened from the blast. Ahead she could see nothing but blackness. Beside her was the hollow breathing of Hook, who sounded like an old furnace kicking out heat. He wiped a film of dust and sweat from his face.

"Did you end it?" he asked quietly in the dark. Annabel couldn't see him at all, and only realized it once she caught herself nodding in reply.

"Yes," she finally said in a rough gravelly whisper, "Deacon was there, at the end. He saved me. He saved us all."

"Always a good man," Hook said quietly. Annabel heard a clicking sound and Hook cursed quietly.

"Do you still have your guns?" he asked.

"I do."

"Are you spent? Your ammunition?" he said.

"Yes. Everything. Why would you…" Annabel realized what he wanted the cartridges for and swallowed hard.

"I don't want to starve blind in the dark, sheriff," Hook said with grim resignation, "Check the kid. He lifted a few rounds from one of the dead ones before the things went mad."

Annabel choked back a sob.

"Why did you stay? Why did you *wait*?"

"We couldn't leave you to that thing, Annabel," Hook replied, "We each decided before you had even made it all the way down to the pit, I think. I wasn't about to leave you behind, and neither was he."

Annabel splayed her arms out in the dark, feeling for the marshal with tears running down her face. She felt the crook of his elbow or knee through the roughened and torn fabric of his suit and pulled aside his jacket to retrieve his revolver, only to find his hand meeting hers instead.

"Hey there," he muttered in the dark, struggling to speak "I'm not seeing a badge. What gives you the right to take a man's iron?"

Annabel laughed and lowered her head down, touching her forehead to his.

"Marshal, I'm so sorry it had to end like this. I don't want it to be over without telling you that you're the most stubborn, arrogant, foolhardy man I've ever met," she whispered.

"I love you too, Anna," he whispered back. She felt him shift underneath her, and his hand pulled something from his pocket. Even in the pitch darkness, Annabel closed her eyes.

A scratching popping noise broke the brief silence after he spoke. Not the sound of a gunshot, but of a match being struck. Annabel's eyes strained to see his face, and she stopped crying all at once as soon as her eyes adjusted.

The passage was still intact. The tiny flame from the match revealed that the dynamite had only blown out a portion of the entrance and the oil lamps nearby. Behind the rubble the marshal was lying on was a space just large enough for them to crawl through to reach the antechamber that led to the surface. Once they had left the passage behind, they could return to seal off the chamber of death beyond the mine shaft here, sealing away the horrors below.

The marshal craned his neck to look at the opening and he scoffed before being seized with a coughing fit.

"Fancy that," he began before coughing robbed him of his speech, "It looks like that dynamite was fouled after all."

Hook smiled in the matchlight and shook his head, not believing the luck of it all. As the match ran down, he saw Annabel move closer to the marshal before the light went out, and the passage was quiet for a moment.

Seconds later another match was lit, and Annabel helped the marshal reach the opening to climb out before she moved to help

Hook. The old man got to his feet by his own power, and together they left the horrors of Emmet Mine behind them.

Chapter XXIII

Outside in the woods the darkness seemed less real now. Whether that was due to Annabel's time spent underground or to something else, she couldn't say. It did feel to her that a kind of peace had come over the forest, and the three of them walked through the woods breathing clean, free air as if it were ambrosia of the gods.

None among their party, not even the marshal, spoke a word until the forest was behind them. They reached their mounts and were not surprised in the slightest to see that the marshal's steed was idly grazing on the golden prairie grass underneath the azure-gray sky. Hook untethered and mounted his mule while Annabel had to help the marshal into his saddle. She couldn't be sure, but it looked like his ankle may have been broken. Despite his suffering, the man was still smiling gently at her in his own peculiar way, and Annabel smiled back. Once they were mounted, they began the ride back to town.

An hour later on the trail, the marshal was taken by another coughing fit that quickly turned to incredulous laughter.

"What could you possibly be laughing at?" Hook said, wearing a stubborn grin of his own. All of them were feeling that unique and unnamable thrill of being alive, truly alive, after a near brush with certain doom.

"Mr. Jeffries is going to have to bill my office for the thread he's going to need to patch us all up," the marshal coughed, "I am rightly torn to pieces, and you both look like old quilts the dog got ahold of."

"Says the man with the face painted in blood," Hook quipped.

"That's just my darker complexion in this light, Mr. Hook," he said, pulling a handkerchief from his pocket to wipe his face, only to find to his dismay it was also stained a deep reddish black.

Annabel said nothing, still overcome with emotion. She feared even trying to talk about what had just happened, or what she had seen over the last weeks would cause her to experience some kind of mental breakdown. Instead she focused on her surroundings. The golden and tawny grasses of the prairie, the thin wisps of smoke from the distant town's chimneys, and the churning sky that swam with the blues and violets of the deep sea.

As day became night, the trio made camp near where they had set down the day before. The marshal, after being helped from his saddle, could scarcely even throw his huckster's grin to either Annabel or Hook before he was fast asleep on the ground. He slept loudly and soundly and coughed in his sleep. Annabel reached to wake him while Hook was preparing the coffee, and the old man shook his head.

"Leave him be, lass. The man had a hard day. If there's any man who has earned a trip to the world of warm and safe dreams, there he lies."

Annabel hesitated before moving her hand away.

"This is the second time I've seen him like this," she said, "I hate it. I hate that this is the life he chose."

"Men like the marshal and Deacon live for this. The moment we're having right now. Emerging victorious over something profaned and abominable. He'll wake and heal and head back east to give his report to a deputy marshal to record, and then he'll do it again."

"*Again*?" Annabel said, "This was enough horror for three lifetimes. He'll just do it again?"

"Until he's dead," Hook answered, taking off his hat and dabbing a bit of cloth at a wound on his pate.

"That's insane."

"Sanity doesn't enter much into the thinking of a man like that," Hook explained, "For what it's worth, I think it's better that way. The frontier needs men and women like him. Folks that ride out against impossible things from campfire stories that live in the dark."

Annabel looked down at the badge she had recovered from Deacon, the flames of the campfire caught on the edges of the star and runes on its surface. Hook peered over to see what it was, and Annabel held the badge out to the old man.

"It was Deacon's," she said, "I don't know why I took it, but it just seemed *wrong* to leave it there. I think he'd want you to have it."

Hook reached for the badge across the fire and stopped himself as his fingertips were inches away. Slowly, he withdrew his hand without the badge.

"Deacon doesn't want for anything anymore," Hook looked into Annabel's eyes, "Deacon is dead. He died years ago when that thing first took him. But you brought him back to save the frontier one last time. If anything, that badge belongs to you."

"Mr. Hook, I can't keep this."

"Leave the mister out of it," he said gruffly, "You've proved yourself more capable a marshal than myself or the man who is snoring yonder. You had no stake in this to ride out with us, no stake to save the marshal after your first trip into the mine. You've got grit, Annabel Hawke. Oath or no oath, I'll count you as one of the best the order has ever seen until the day I die."

Looking down at the badge again, Annabel saw herself in its surface. Coated in ash and blood she felt reborn somehow and didn't know what to make of the fact. Not wanting to linger on it, she put the badge away.

Hook poured the last of the coffee, all the grounds had been used up the night before and handed Annabel a tin cup of it. Both drank quietly throughout the night, drifting in and out of brief sleep as they watched fire burn down to cinder. Before long, the black clouds overhead became tinged with the tangerine pink of the approaching dawn. The storm that had been building the day before seemed to have dissipated before it ever began.

Hook finished the last drop of coffee and began breaking camp alongside Annabel, who moved in slow motion through the routine, lost in thought. While readying to wake the marshal, she stopped herself.

"What happens now?" she asked Hook, "Will you go back out to your cabin on the prairie?"

The thin old man's eyes drifted to the western horizon, then came back to look at Ganndo Valley in the distance.

"I've had enough of guilt and solitude," he said slowly, "If you'll have me, I'd like to settle in town here. It seems like a good place as any to spend what years I've got left."

Annabel laughed, almost not believing him.

"What will you do to pass the time?"

"I have a lot of drinking and card playing to catch up on, I'm sure. On top of that, I'll have to re-learn how to be a civilized man. Of course, a man can't spend all his time with leisure. I don't suppose you're looking for a deputy?"

"You wouldn't be the first marshal I've considered for the job," she said with a smile that was somewhat sad. She looked again at the marshal, still fast asleep.

"I don't want to wake him," she said, her voice sounding a thousand miles away from her thoughts.

"When he wakes, you need to tell him how you really feel," Hook said, "Life is short that way. You never regret what you said, but you'll regret what you didn't say. I can't promise he'll give it all up to be with you, but he does love you. That much is clear. Help me get him on his saddle. I'll tether his mount to the mule."

Annabel and Hook gingerly lifted the man onto his steed, and the three rode the rest of the way back to town with the light of dawn ahead of them in the east.

Their arrival in town was a blur to Annabel. It drifted by as if in a dream. They rode past the town's edge and were spotted by Old Bill, who had assembled a makeshift lookout tower out of a ladder and what looked like a tabletop ripped from the saloon. He ran to greet them and, in a flash, had whistled for young Colm to fetch Mr. Jeffries, and to get Mrs. Mattingly to get a start on what he called a "buffalo breakfast."

Annabel watched Colm and Mr. Abernathy help carry the marshal away with Mr. Jeffries close at hand. At the same time the sheriff found herself and Hook whisked away to the hotel by Roy Mattingly, who swore up and down she was the best sheriff who had ever lived bar none, and went on ad nauseum about her exploits being sent to the paper as she ate a pile of scrambled eggs in a daze.

After retiring to the hotel's drawing room for coffee, Annabel found the comfort of her armchair to be too much, and in an instant, she was asleep, safe among the townsfolk she had delivered from destruction.

Chapter XXIV

Annabel awoke not knowing where she was.

She blinked her eyes open slowly to see soft white light lazily floating through soft curtains into a room she did not recognize. The room was painted a soft red, and there were fine wood furnishings arrayed around the place. A wardrobe, a chest, and a small table beside the enormous bed she found herself in, with a small white vase with a lavender bloom resting in it.

She sat up in the bed to find her clothes had been replaced with a nightgown, and her hand, her hip, and her head were bandaged. Taking a deep breath and fighting a bout of vertigo, she threw the covers off of her body and pulled on the boots beside the bed. They weren't her boots, but rather were a fine brown leather that was polished and new. With unsteady steps that pained her hip, Annabel walked to the door of the room and walked out into the hallway.

She was in the hotel. Turning around she could see the number on the door in brass, and the small wooden label handing from twine over the doorknob that warned visitors to not disturb whoever was inside. She walked past other rooms to the corner of the hall that led to the stairs, and shakily navigated her way down them.

The drawing room of the hotel was empty, save for one occupant seated at a small table near the window, watching the people outside going about their morning as if nothing had happened. It was Hook, wearing a new navy-blue jacket, resting his hand on a new white Stetson hat on the table. Before him was a white plate colored a deep purple at one edge, where jam flecked with biscuit crumbs had stuck to it. Hook's napkin, knife, and fork lay neatly beside it, reflecting the sun. At the sound of Annabel's boots thumping on the ground he turned to her and immediately turned away after seeing her state of dress.

"Blast it, Sheriff, I know you're not the most ladylike woman, but you still *are* a woman. You've got an entire wardrobe filled with new clothes upstairs. Make yourself decent."

"What happened?" she asked, ignoring the old man and taking a seat across from him. He kept his face covered.

"Hook, please," she said, annoyed and slightly frustrated. The old man turned in his seat and removed his jacket before thrusting it over to her.

"Put this on, at least. Someone could see you."

Annabel pulled the jacket on and felt it was almost too small even for her. Hook seemed satisfied with it and uncovered his eyes.

"Can I get an answer now? Or do I need your hat and trousers too?"

"You fell asleep in the chair while Mr. Jeffries was asking about your injuries. Old Bill had been fighting to keep everyone out of the hotel, seeing as just about everyone wanted to know what happened with the 'bandits,' at the mine."

"Then what?" she urged him, still not satisfied with his answer.

"That sentimentality after our near-death experience sure didn't stick around with you for long, did it?" Hook asked, waving his hand to slow her down, "Jeffries patched you up. Mrs. Mattingly gave you that nightgown and had myself and Roy help you upstairs to bed. Earlier this morning some fop from the general store, Rawlins I think his name was, came by with a whole mess of clothes for you. Duncan brought a new gun belt and a fresh iron for you. Mr. Abernathy from the saloon says your money's no good there anymore, you drink for free, so on and so forth."

"Really?" she asked, "They did all that for *me*?"

"I doubt it'll stick, folks forget turns like this after a while, but yes they did it for you. By the time the fellow from the paper showed up I gave him a pretty mean snarl and told him off. It's just been me and the Mattinglys here all day."

"I'm sure you've suffered quite a bit there," Annabel said with a smirk, "Mrs. Mattingly loves a lawman."

"You hush," Hook grumbled with a smile, "After this I'll have to put in real work to keep these folks from being so familiar with me."

Annabel looked out the window at the townsfolk, milling about the streets just as they did the first day the marshal rode into town. She found herself amazed that for all of them life went on just as it did before, with the events of the last few days being reduced to an interesting story that got more and more mundane the longer it was told. After a time, her thoughts wandered back to the marshal, and how he looked at them with such admiration and wonder that first day he arrived. She looked at Hook and saw he wasn't smiling any longer.

"Hook, what's the matter?" she asked him, leaning on her elbows. The thin elderly man bowed his head and sighed.

"I fear I am just at a loss for words at the moment."

Looking at his drawn features, Annabel put her hand on his reassuringly, feeling the warmth of the sun on her arm as she did so. She looked over her shoulder to the door, and then outside. Down the street she could see Mr. Jeffries' office, and thought for a moment.

"Where's the marshal?" the sheriff asked. Hook sighed and pulled his hand gently away from hers. He didn't answer. Annabel's face became pale, and she leaned back in her chair.

"Did he make it? I mean, is he still alive?" she asked with a slight quiver in her voice. The parlor was silent as Hook looked at his plate.

"He's alive," the old man said to the sheriff's relief. Yet still, Hook looked melancholy. He took a deep breath and cleared his throat, mustering enough courage to speak as plainly as he could to the young woman.

"Sheriff, I have something for you," he said somberly. Hook pointed at the inside pocket of the jacket she now wore, "In there."

Laughing uncomfortably, Annabel reached her fingers into the jacket pocket and withdrew a sealed cream-colored envelope, sealed with a small wax star set into a ring of runes.

"What is this?" she asked. Hook bowed his head and held his hook in his good hand.

"It's from the marshal. I couldn't tell you what it is, I didn't open it," he murmured, clearing his throat, "I think I hear some folks outside. I'd better clear them out. You go on upstairs and get dressed properly now. People will want to talk to you."

Annabel didn't hear anyone, but understood the man was trying to give her some time alone. Hook rose abruptly from the table and planted his hat on his head before walking to the door and heading outside, leaving Annabel alone with the envelope.

She ran her finger over the seal that mirrored the badge the marshal wore and contemplated not opening the thing at all. After a moment of thought on the matter, she picked up the knife from Hook's breakfast and wiped a bit of jam from it with his napkin before opening it and withdrawing a letter.

The letter was written in a careful, neat scrawl that got more cramped and ugly as it went on. It was rife with missteps and choices in tone, and Annabel could at once tell the marshal had a difficult time composing it. It was very much in the style of the marshal's hand from what Annabel had seen in his little notebook he carried. Lifting it to the light, she read it.

~~My dearest Annabel,~~

~~Dear Sheriff,~~

Anna,

I am a poor man when it comes to goodbyes, and an even worse example of a writer when it comes to letters. I never found much use in it outside of the occasional request for material or support from my offices, and in truth, I cannot recall ever writing something like this before.

The past few weeks have been the most harrowing of my life. As a marshal you see and experience things that truly challenge

225

your ability to remain human. A man goes looking for monsters in all things, and soon begins to see them in all things. I have spent my time wearing the badge building a veneer behind which I can hide and preserve my humanity while doing the things I am called to do, and I confess on this particular ride I felt that veneer beginning to peel at the edges.

What helped me hold on, and what helped me find my purpose and conviction again, was you. I never before have known a braver, stronger, more noble soul, and I very much doubt I shall ever know another that even holds a candle to it.

When you offered me an opportunity to stay in Ganndo Valley with you I nearly took it. The thought of leaving this behind and settling the frontier as an honest lawman serving an honest community felt like a dream. But down in the mine, and on the trail leading to it, I saw in you that very fire that the marshals desperately needed in its service to defend places like the valley from the forces like that which rested beneath it until yesterday.

I would never ask that you join the marshals. In truth I hope you forget them soon after I am gone.

Seeing you reminded me of what I fought for, and what I must continue to fight for. It is with ~~some~~ great regret that I inform you in this letter that I am leaving the valley, and am likely already rail-bound to return to the office back east to report on this case and begin the next one after a short time of rest and contemplation.

It is not lightly I leave the frontier and Ganndo Valley behind me. The people here are a gift, and they live on because of the commitment to the marshals that I must preserve, and your commitment and love for the community you must protect.

Please know that despite my leaving, I love you Annabel Hawke.

Yours most truly,

M

Alone and crestfallen, Annabel read the letter again. She thought back to what Mr. Jeffries had said to her in the saloon before she rode out to the mine about her and the marshal having parts to play. The marshal had made his choice. Sitting on the bed in the hotel room, Annabel wondered what choice she would have made if given a chance. Despite everything, she couldn't bring herself to hate the man for leaving. Whatever had been between them, be it desperate emotions in a desperate time, or something more, was gone now. The letter she now held was all that was left of whatever might have been.

Folding the letter gently in her hand, Annabel took a deep breath. In a way it surprised her, she had guessed the marshal would have left without saying goodbye at all, but the letter almost made it worse. After everything, he was still a marshal, faceless and nameless. He had told her he loved her, and still did not bother giving her a name to remember him by. Setting the paper onto the table beside the bed roughly, she stood to approach the room's window.

Days ago, armed men stood outside this very window on the balcony firing at her. The men and women down in the street who now walked in the sun might have been beneath the earth, slaving for a monster if not for herself, Hook, and the marshal. Looking at the people, Annabel knew the marshal was right to leave the way he did. It would have been impossible to say goodbye to him face to face.

Annabel was morosely thankful that she hadn't told him that she loved him. Knowing that she might have said it, and then knowing he left would have been a venomous wound.

Walking to the wardrobe, Annabel pulled the doors open gently and surveyed the items within, looking for something to do with her hands to take her mind off of the matter. Inside she pulled out a fresh pair of blue jeans and a button-down shirt and got dressed. A new stalker hat rested atop a shelf in the wardrobe, and Annabel put it on before fastening a new leather gun belt over her hips, feeling a sense of purpose and pride begin to wash away the last traces of sorrow from her heart.

It was for the best that he and his strange world were gone from this place. What Hook said was also true. In short time, folks who traveled here that once may have disappeared would be settling down soon, and word would travel like lightning once it was discovered how much silver was down in Emmet Mine. Annabel knew that in the coming days Ganndo valley would need its sheriff.

And the frontier would always need its marshals.

Acknowledgements

Preparing this book and actually writing it were both long affairs, to which I owe many people a great deal of thanks for.

This entire thing started life as a short horror story, maybe sixteen pages long, where a man from a shadowy organization comes to town and discovers something is amiss. After the he is confronted with the horrors in the valley, he reveals to the local law what is happening before shooting her and deciding to burn the whole valley down to destroy the evil lurking there. Thankfully, that version of the story never came to pass, thanks in part to encouragement from so many people who read my first book. Their love and support are directly responsible for the book you now hold in your hands or see on your screen.

Lorraine Rice was the first person to call me to talk about my first book. Her excitement and enthusiasm really helped provide me with confidence to give this thing another try. Steven Engledow pushed to get that very same work into the Sarasota County library in Florida, and in doing so checked off an item on my bucket list that I didn't even know was there. His support while I was working on this book was tremendous, and he offered me very solid advice when I was feeling like it wasn't good enough for print.

A number of good people read the teaser for the manuscript, and offered suggestions, encouragement, and information about details and tone. I am especially grateful to Katherine Norberg, who read not only that but looked over my first printing of my first book and gave it a fantastic read-through to help clean up and tone that book. Without her, people would still be pointing out errors to me. I also want to thank my friends at *The Geekery* here in Kansas, for providing me with feedback and encouragement while I was writing this and helped dispel the myth that "no one cares about yeehaw adventures in 2020." Recently I've been thinking a lot about my grandfather and how much I think he'd like this one, even if it gets a bit strange sometimes. His love for westerns was catching, and both myself and my father have inherited it from him. In many ways he's solely to blame for my interest in the genre, and in butterscotch pie.

I want to thank my family, James, Julie, Lindsay, and Mary Kate who loved me and tolerated me while I was bringing up the details of the story even while at the same time considering not finishing it at all. If no one reads this book other than them, I'd still have the best audience in the entire world.

Lastly, I want to thank my editor and wife, Marja. I'm lucky to have her as an editor, and I cannot even begin to express how lucky I am to know her as my best friend, companion, and partner. She has been uncomplaining, patient, and calm while I stressed over how things would read or sound, and for helping Annabel and the marshal seem that much more real. I made her sit through so many westerns and many, many nights of talking things through on this book while flip-flopping on actually putting it out there. You are everything to me.

I love you. -Patrick Cullen, September 2020.

Made in the USA
Las Vegas, NV
26 September 2021